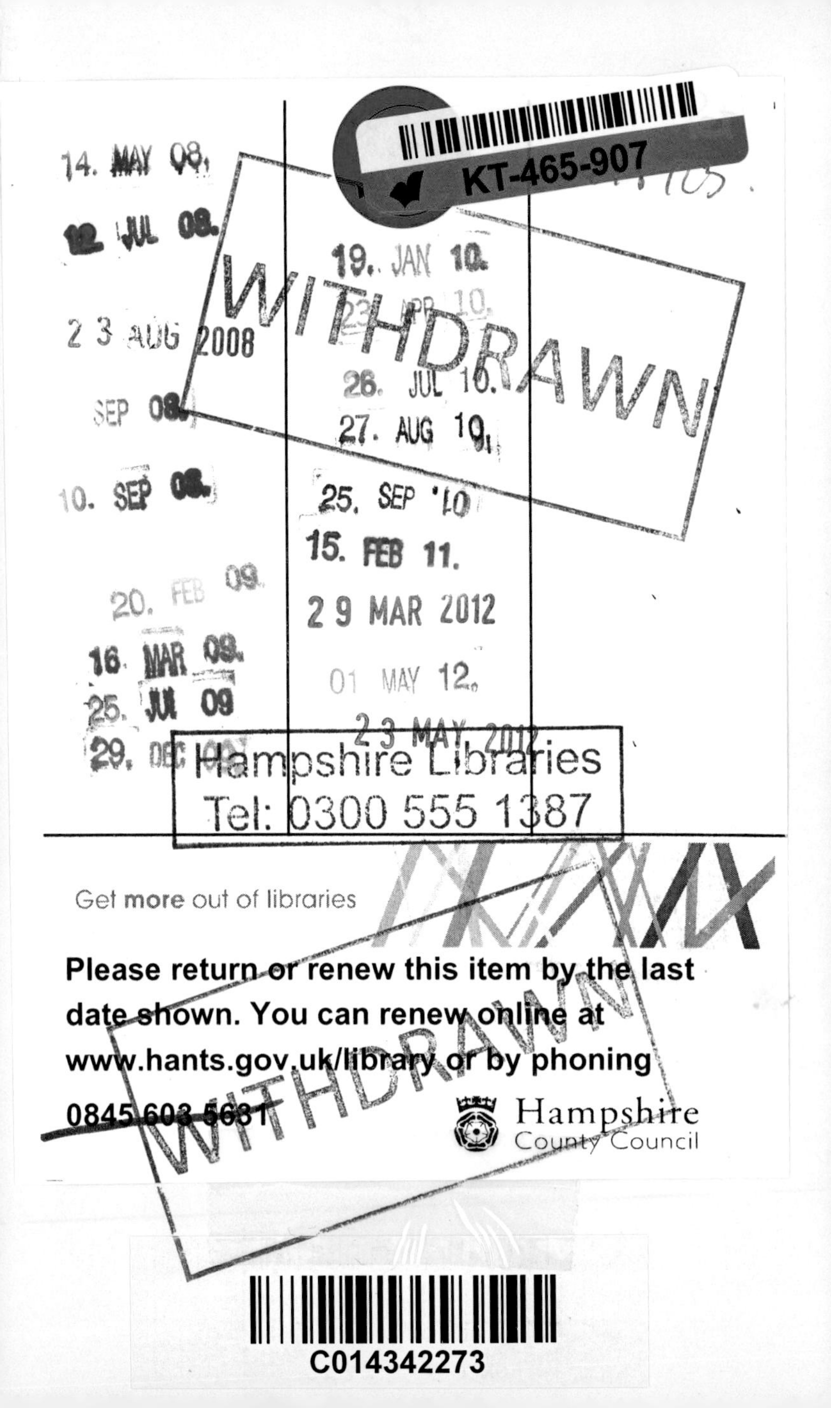
KT-465-907
14. MAY 08.
12. JUL 08.
23 AUG 2008
SEP 08.
10. SEP 08.
20. FEB 09.
16. MAR 09.
25. JUL 09
29. DEC
19. JAN 10.
23 APR 10.
26. JUL 10.
27. AUG 10.
25. SEP '10
15. FEB 11.
29 MAR 2012
01 MAY 12.
23 MAY 2012
WITHDRAWN
Hampshire Libraries
Tel: 0300 555 1387
Get more out of libraries
Please return or renew this item by the last date shown. You can renew online at www.hants.gov.uk/library or by phoning 0845 603 5631
WITHDRAWN
Hampshire County Council
C014342273

Six Days to Sundown

After a marauding band of killers leaves Casey Storm afoot, his horse shot out from under him, he is forced to brave a high plains blizzard. Stumbling upon a wagon train of Montana settlers he falls in with them to help them fight their way toward the new settlement of Sundown. But an army of gunmen hired by a land-hungry madman dogs their trail.

The pursuing killers, approaching winter and an indifferent army all combine to block the wagon train's progress and any hope the settlers hold for a new life. Casey alone refuses to give up the battle even when the opposing elements collide explosively. Now the dwindling calendar leaves them only six bloody days to reach Sundown.

Will they win through and claim their land?

By the same author

The Devil's Canyon
The Drifter's Revenge
West of Tombstone
On The Wapiti Range
Rolling Thunder
The Bounty Killers

Six Days to Sundown

Owen G. Irons

ROBERT HALE · LONDON

First published in Great Britain 2008

ISBN 978-0-7090-8532-4

Robert Hale Limited
Clerkenwell House
Clerkenwell Green
London EC1R 0HT

www.halebooks.com

Typeset by
Derek Doyle & Associates, Shaw Heath
Printed and bound in Great Britain by
Antony Rowe Limited, Wiltshire

ONE

Montana was bleeding. To the west, the sky cast scattered colors against the leaden sky, like reflections from a shattered stained-glass window. Deep umber, washy violet and hazy crimson streaked the clouds and sketched crazy shadows across the land. To the east, the far-running sky was steel-dust gray, cold and somber. A ground mist was beginning to rise from the long prairie flats as the pursuers spurred their horses forward.

Casey Storm lay head downward in the coulée where he had faltered, stumbled and plunged into its sandy depths. He could do nothing to help himself, to lift himself up, to try to scramble onward. His race was run and he had lost to the Shadow Riders.

Why they wanted to kill him he still did not know. He only knew that they would do that if they found him again.

His own horse, the big buckskin he had been riding for three years, had nearly run itself to death before a chance shot from his pursuers stopped the big horse in its tracks and sent it rolling head over heels with Casey given only a split second to kick free of the stirrups and leap from the tumbling animal. He had managed to keep his grip on his Henry repeating rifle, but there were only three rounds remaining in its tube magazine, hardly enough to hold off the Shadow Riders. At a rough count there had been ten or twelve of them when they first emerged from the shadowy haze of twilight time. All of them wore black slickers and were faceless in the gloom.

Casey had reined in, lifting a hand to the men, hoping to find trail information and possibly even a camp with hot coffee, his own supplies being nearly depleted. Instead, when the riders were still fifty yards away, one of them had shouldered his rifle and begun to fire. Prudence inspired Casey to slap spurs to the big buckskin's flanks and begin an all-out run across the long-grass plains, rifle bullets pursuing him.

After his horse had gone down, Casey had run on in a crouch, his breath coming in short gasps, his heart racing wildly until at last he had tripped over an unseen root and fallen sprawled against the sandy bluff of the coulée.

He could hear them coming still, their horses now

at a walk, knowing that he was on foot. He could hear muttered words being exchanged, though none came clearly. The sky continued to darken and the colors faded to a uniform grayness, tending toward blue-black. Never had a man prayed more for night to envelop the world, for the icy darkness to settle than did Casey. He did not move, look back, try to position himself for a last desperate struggle. He lay face down in the sand as the shadows mingled and pooled beneath the willow brush that clotted the coulée bottom. He knew the Shadow Riders would kill him without hesitation if they found him.

They had already proved that.

Who they could be, why they wanted him dead he could not guess. He had only recently ridden into the Montana country out of Cheyenne, Wyoming, where things had gotten a little too tight for him, partly because of his own carelessness. But this band of nameless, faceless men had swarmed upon him without cause like a group of enraged hostile Indians, and there had to be a reason for it.

Casey wondered at that moment as the sky faded and he lay helplessly against the cold earth if he would live long enough to discover what that reason was.

Now, lying as still as a dead man he could hear them speaking in low tones, hear nervous horses pawing at the earth on the rim of the coulée, shaking their heads so that their bridle chains rattled. One man's voice was appreciably louder than the others, reckless and angry.

'We're not going to find him on this night! Probably broke his neck when the horse rolled.'

'Shut up, Earl!' a second man hissed. 'We've got to find him.'

'You couldn't find a mountain on a night like this. Besides, it's going to rain. I tell you he broke his neck.'

The second man responded crossly. 'Keep your voice down. You'll make targets of us all if he's lurking out there.'

One of the riders had walked his pony so near to the edge of the coulée that a few small rocks followed by a trickle of sand washed down across Casey where he lay.

The man called Earl laughed loudly. 'Targets? If there's a man living who could pick us out in this blackness, I'd give him a medal!'

'Just quiet down,' the other said impatiently. 'We'll keep looking. McCoy wants him dead, you know that.'

'And what McCoy wants he gets,' Earl answered bitterly.

'So long as he's paying my wages – and yours.'

Their horses rested now, seeing nothing ahead of them but the pitch blackness of the night plains, Casey heard them turn their mounts and ride away. He had been confining his breathing to slow, labored puffs. Now, as the sounds of the Shadow Riders dimmed and were swallowed by the night, he sat up, wrapped his arms around his knees and took in a series of deep, resuscitating gulps of cold air. The small effort brought stabbing pain to his side and he realized that he had probably broken a rib or two in the tumble from the buckskin's saddle.

Very cautiously he rose to his feet, looking around carefully, listening intently. The riders had gone, but it was possible they had left a watcher behind. Seeing no one, hearing nothing, he started down the flank of the sandy wash toward the brush-clotted bottom. In the darkness he fought his way through the knots of willow brush and sumac to the far side, climbed painfully up the opposite bank and on to level land again, his arms and face scratched, his ribs aching in protest.

The few words he had heard exchanged between the riders had done nothing to illuminate him. He knew no man named McCoy, so why would he – whoever he was – want Casey dead? He only knew that he had blundered into trouble and that he wanted now to get as far away from it as possible.

Trouble, after all, was the reason he had left Cheyenne. A man hopes that trouble can be left behind, but it seemed to cling to Casey Storm like a plaster. Standing on the bank of the coulée, his rifle in his hand, he looked up into the darkness, but the moon was hidden in the tumult of the skies and no stars winked on to give him his bearings. Utilizing the prevailing wind as his rough compass, he began trudging slowly westward. Hatless, injured and lost, he walked on through the cold Montana night.

An hour later it began to rain.

Lightning illuminated the crooked sky and thunder racketed so near at hand that it was deafening. The rain fell in silver pellets, driving against Casey's shoulders and face with such violence that he was tempted to curl up embryonically against the cold, sodden earth and let the night have its way. To do so would have been suicidal; there was no way of knowing how long the angry storm would continue to rage. The temperature was dropping rapidly. He had to find shelter, any rough refuge. A thicket to cut the biting wind, a hollow log! Anything at all.

He had heard all the stories about these north plains storms which rose like angry beasts and could blanket the world in minutes with snow, of the ten-foot drifts and men who had sacrificed their ponies, cut them open to crawl inside of them for their body heat in a last desperate attempt to survive. It was not snowing, not yet, but these tales manifested themselves luridly in his mind as he struggled on against the cold, buckshot rain and grappling wind. His boots groped their way forward. The earth underneath their soles was growing sodden and slick. His head was bowed necessarily. The rain was a driving, blinding force.

He staggered more than walked on. He had no sense of direction and little energy left. He could not defeat the elements by will alone. Once he did stop, lifted his face to the tumult of the Montana sky and shouted, 'Damn you, McCoy! Whoever you are, I curse you.'

He stumbled on then, his legs leaden, effectively blinded by the dark of the storm. Casey walked for miles – or was that only in his mind? Time and distance had lost their meaning as the rain continued to fall, the lightning to crackle with blinding brilliance at one moment; in the next allowing the night to sink back into Stygian darkness.

He halted abruptly. Stumbling on, his feet frozen, lungs filled with cold air that made each breath seem life-threatening, he had not noticed that the wind was now at his back! Had he been wandering in circles? He knew this could happen even to experienced trailsmen in territory they knew well. Casey did not know this land intimately. He paused, wiping the cold water from his eyes. The storm had shifted direction – that was all there was to it. Or so he convinced himself. At any rate there was no choice but to continue, to seek shelter. Or to lie down and die.

Some time near midnight it began to snow.

The temperature plunged with appalling suddenness, harsh sleet began to cut at Casey's face like icy daggers. Then the snow began. Huge, fluffy flakes at first and then a constant, impenetrable veil of twisting, wind-driven snow. Casey bowed his head and plunged on once again, seeking shelter, any poor shelter.

With his head bowed to the forces of the storm, in the near-complete darkness he walked directly into a solid, waist-high object and stumbled back, gasping in pain as fire shot through his injured ribs. Like a blind man seeking, he stuck out searching fingers and found the object again. It was the lowered plank tailgate of a wagon.

Peering into the wrath of the storm he could make out the distinctive shape of a covered wagon's canvas roof and hear the fabric snapping against the iron bands supporting it. Abandoned? Occupied? Either way it made no difference to Casey Storm. He shouted out as loudly as he could above the battering rush of the storm and painfully clambered up on to the tailgate and into the wagon.

'Come one inch nearer and I'll blow you apart,' a man's voice said with soft assurance.

'I'm hurt and half-frozen to death.'

'It's a tough life,' the quiet voice responded.

The thinnest gleam of light from somewhere showed the man in silhouette to Casey and winked briefly on the barrel of a long gun aimed at his mid=section. 'Why are you still here?' the stranger demanded, when Casey made no move to depart.

'I'll perish out there for sure,' Casey said, with more

calm then he felt. 'I suppose it's no worse to die quick from a bullet than to freeze to death in a blizzard.'

'Are you asking for mercy! A McCoy rider!' the man in the shadows laughed.

'I'm not one of them. They ambushed me and left-me afoot,' Casey said.

'I can't take the chance of believing you,' the man replied. The sound of the rife being cocked was clear and sharp in the night even with the wind continuing to batter the flimsy canvas cover of the wagon and the weird moaning of the storm.

'For God's sake, Dad,' a second voice said, invading in the stand-off. 'At least hear the man out!'

The voice was a woman's, a young woman's. Casey heard the rustling of heavy robes and sensed rather than saw the young lady sit up in her night bed.

'We can't descend to McCoy's level.'

A match was struck and a candle lit on the floorboard of the covered wagon. By its flickering light Casey saw the grim, long-jawed man in a buffalo coat holding his Sharps rifle, his scowl deep and pouched eyes fierce. The woman who had struck the match and lighted the candle was tiny. Her dark hair was in disarray around her shoulders. Her eyes, too large for her face, were wide with concern or simple curiosity. She held her blankets just below her chin protectively.

'He doesn't look that dangerous to me,' the girl said around a heavy yawn.

'I have only one question for you,' her father said to Casey. 'If you give me the wrong answer I'll plug you. Is your name Deveraux?'

Casey's lips narrowed. What answer did the man want? Which was the correct answer to save his life? He decided on honesty.

'I've never heard the name before,' he replied honestly.

'Then you're the wrong man,' the older man said grimly, raising his rifle butt to his shoulder.

The girl reached out through the smoky light of the wagon's interior and pressed the rifle barrel down.

'Dad,' she said, 'he can't help it if he's not Stan Deveraux.' Returning her wide dark eyes to Casey Storm, she said, 'I still don't think he looks dangerous enough to kill. Let him tell his story.'

The storm raged on outside as Casey, at a gesture, lowered himself to sit cross-legged on the planks of the wagon bed. The candle guttered and scattered shifting shadows across the white canvas roof. Quietly, Casey told them what had happened, how he had been jumped by a group of men – one of whom's name was Earl – and heard them talking about McCoy having sent them to kill him. 'They killed my horse and left me to die,' he concluded.

The man with the rifle ran his fingers through his longish salt-and-pepper hair and frowned with one corner of his mouth. 'They must have thought you were Deveraux,' he said after some reflection.

'You believe me?' Casey asked with relief.

'I disbelieve you less,' the older man answered dryly. 'That's far from saying you're welcome here.'

'Do you mind if I ask just who Stan Deveraux is? And just who this McCoy is?' Casey said. 'If it's not my business, just say so. But I can see that I've walked into trouble and I don't even know what it's about.'

'You're right,' the man with the rifle answered. 'It's not your business. If you've no hand to play, there's no need for you to understand the game.'

'All right,' Casey shrugged. Outside thunder boomed again as close lightning illuminated the shadowed wagon. 'Whatever you say.'

'So long as I've got this .50 Sharps, you are correct,' the old man said. 'It is whatever I say. Now I suggest you just be on your way to wherever it is you're going.'

'Tonight!' Casey was aghast. 'A man would die out there on a night like this.'

'Could happen,' the old man said without sympathy. 'Should have stayed out of the north country if you weren't equipped for it. This is nothing compared to our deep winter storms. I'd say you have a good chance of lasting till morning.'

'Dad?' the girl spoke again. 'You've said many times when men came calling that you wouldn't turn a dog out on a night like this. Why are you doing it now?'

'Why?' the man replied peevishly. 'Because we don't know what we've got here – a snake, a wolf, a back-shooter . . . and I've got you in here, Daughter.'

'He still doesn't look dangerous to me,' the girl said, and yawning again, she rolled up in her blankets against the chill of the night.

The girl's father continued to glare at Casey Storm and Casey lifted both hands and said, 'I'm going to make a move now. Don't get over-anxious with that buffalo gun.'

The man did not reply although his frown deepened as Casey reached under the skirt of his coat and very slowly, using only his thumb and index finger, removed his Colt revolver from its holster. This he slid across the floor toward the feet of the mistrustful stranger. Using a boot he nudged his Henry repeating rifle in the same direction. The watching man lifted one eyebrow, but he did not move a muscle.

'I'd die out there tonight, and you know it,' Casey said in answer to the questioning stare. 'Let me curl up in a corner of the wagon and I'll pull out in the morning.' Without waiting for an answer, Casey withdrew into the farthest corner of the covered wagon and curled up in a tight ball, using his hat as a pillow. There was a movement behind him but he did not open his eyes to discover the cause. Then a blanket was thrown over him and the older man growled, 'All right then, damn you! Marly was right, I guess; she usually is – you don't look that dangerous to me either.'

With the morning the Shadow Riders returned.

TWO

When Casey Storm awoke, stiff, sore and disoriented, sunlight was streaming in brightly through the flaps of the covered wagon's canvas. Sitting up in his blanket, he found himself alone. His host – if he could be called that – and the girl were gone. Surprisingly, Casey's rifle and Colt revolver were near at hand on the plank floor of the wagon. He checked their loads and tucked the revolver back into its holster. Rubbing his head he rose unsteadily. The tumble he had taken had not seemed that painful at the time, but overnight muscles had stiffened, bruises had deepened.

He heard the sounds of movement outside, of horses stamping, people speaking in confident if not cheerful voices, the bark of a dog. Apparently then, when he had arrived in the snowstorm of the previous night he had stumbled not upon a single wagon, but into a camp of settlers. He folded the blanket he had been given, picked up his rifle and opened the canvas flaps.

Squinting into the sunlight, brilliant in the blue sky and mirrorlike as it reflected off the new-fallen snow, he saw that he had been right. There were dozens of men and women, a few children at their breakfasts on wagon tailgates, hunched around low-burning fires, leading teams of horses to their harnesses. Perhaps, then, his luck had finally changed for the better. Surely someone in this group would be willing to let him travel along with them if he offered some assistance in return.

Casey had to sit down on the tailgate and swing himself carefully to the ground. His battered body could do no more. In other times he would have simply leaped off, confident in his youthful strength. That was before yesterday. Today he felt already old, weary and hungry.

No sooner had his boots touched the ground than people began to pause to look at him, to point him out, to whisper. What sort of camp was this? Were they all as suspicious of strangers as the man he had met last night? Tugging his hat lower against the glare of the morning, he trudged across the camp toward the nearest fire, hoping for a cup of coffee if nothing more. The snow underfoot was already thinning, the ground underneath unfrozen. His boots left muddy imprints behind him as he approached a group of settlers. The young woman turned to meet him.

'Coffee?' Marly asked.

'It's what I was hoping for,' Casey said to the big-eyed girl he had met but not been introduced to the night before. He offered her a smile as she poured a cup from a steaming gallon pot kept warm on the dying fire's embers and offered it to him. Apparently his charm was not working on this particular morning. He received not the slightest hint of a smile in return. She was dressed in a pair of men's black jeans and a flannel shirt. The bulk of a heavy buffalo coat made her appear fuller than she actually was. Casey remembered that much about the previous night's experience. When her blanket had slipped briefly from her shoulders, he had had a glimpse of strong-appearing, but very slight arms. He thanked Marly by name, but she turned away without responding. Her dark hair was done in unusual fashion, separated into two twists, not quite braids, that hung down her back. Perhaps it was all that she had the time to do with it out here, under these conditions.

He was still watching her, sipping at the rapidly cooling coffee in his tin cup when her father came striding into view from around the back of a second wagon. The old man with the big .50 caliber buffalo gun wore a flop hat, half-boots, jeans and a fleece-lined leather jacket. He was quite tall, and though the strands of gray hair that had slipped from under his hat showed him to be of middle years, he was confident in his stride, erect and even rigid in his mannerisms. A former military man? Casey guessed so.

A few men had gathered around father and daughter and, as Casey finished his coffee, he heard a few words: 'No, haven't seen them yet.' 'We'd better get moving soon.' 'Damn this snow . . .' And then the group divided, each man going about his business. Casey stood uneasily near the dead fire, wondering what his next move should be. Unexpectedly Marly's father turned, looked Casey's way and marched directly toward him.

'Jason Landis,' the formerly hostile man said, extending a bony hand which Casey took. 'Sorry about last night, but we've all been a little jittery with what's been going on, and there's my daughter of course. Did I catch your name?'

'Casey Storm,' he was told. The old man's eyes searched Casey's sun-tanned face and quiet pale eyes and nodded.

'I was up and riding with the sunrise, Casey,' Jason Landis told him. 'Checking the backtrail. Never know what McCoy'll do next.' Landis spoke – habitually it seemed – in short, concentrated sentences which strengthened Casey's impression that Landis had once been a soldier, accustomed to snapping out orders rather than holding discussions.

'No sign of them?' Casey asked. Meaning the men he had come to think of as the Shadow Riders.

'Nothing. I rode back as far as the coulée. Didn't

cross it, of course. Saw your horse down. A buckskin, wasn't it? Substantiates your story. Sorry I couldn't expend the time to try retrieving your saddle and goods. We'll have to make do with what we have.'

We? Casey felt like a man who had just been impressd into service. No questions asked. No permission given. Still he felt a wave of relief pass through him. Alone, afoot in this country he would have had no chance of survival. None at all.

'What can I do?' Casey asked, noting that the other settlers were in motion all around him.

'Help Marly hitch the team,' Landis said, still authoritative. Casey smiled inwardly. He was willing to take orders.

The new inductee started back toward the front of the wagon where Marly, practiced in the skill, seemed in little need of his assistance. Four mismatched horses, breathing steam, stamped impatiently, eager, it seemed, to resume their trek.

'Did Father draft you?' she asked, without looking up as she fastened the trace chains.

'So it seems,' Casey answered with a grin.

Marly paused for a moment, straightened up and turned her huge dark eyes on him, measuring Casey Storm. It was difficult to read her expression. She shrugged, wiped her small hands on her jeans and said, 'Well, it beats a firing squad.'

The joke – if that was what it was intended to be – was darkly prophetic, for no sooner had Marly finished speaking than the roar of the guns began.

One of the first bullets slammed into the side of the Landis wagon, gouging out a spray of long splinters. Marly swung around, her large eyes wider than usual. Gaping at him, she said, 'I'll hold the team!'

She started for the wagon box, but before she could reach it, Casey grabbed her arm and pulled her roughly back to the ground. He forced her ahead of him, crawling under the shelter of the wagon bed to the rear. Bellied down in the cold mud, he fixed his sights on the first raider he saw. The in-rider rode a roan horse and wore a black slicker as they all did. He had a bandanna worn as a mask, so Casey didn't see his face as he shot him from his pony's back. He lay still when he hit the snow-streaked earth.

The camp was in chaos. The men, preparing to pack up and start along the trail, were not carrying their rifles; only a few wore handguns. The roar of gunfire was, nevertheless, fierce and deadly from both sides. Casey heard a settler not fifty feet away scream and, glancing through the spokes of the wagon wheel, saw him throw his arms high, perform a grotesque pirouette and fall dead.

The Shadow Riders circled the camp like Indians and then charged directly through its ranks, guns blazing. Casey knew he had only two loads left in his Henry repeater, and cursed grimly when he wasted one of them with an ill-timed shot at a hard-galloping gunman. His third shot was more effective, but only marginally so.

The .44-.40 slug from his long gun tagged one of the raiders high on the shoulder and he rocked in his saddle but did not go down. Casey threw his rifle aside and drew his Colt. Angry now, he crawled from under the wagon, feeling Marly's restraining hand claw at the fabric of his sleeve. He saw another of the settlers curled up against the snow and mud of the campsite, heard a woman scream.

On his feet, Casey braced himself and began firing with deliberation. He managed to tag at least one more of the onrushing raiders. Casey watched him double up and saw the rifle drop from his hand. He managed, nevertheless, to swing his horse away from the battle. A bullet flew past Casey's head and passed through the wagon's interior and he was relieved that he had not let Marly clamber up into the box.

From within the camp perimeter now, the guns of the settlers began to fire with more rapidity and authority. Some of the men had managed to reach their weapons and take up positions of defense. The raiders touched spurs to their horses' flanks and beat a hasty retreat, shots following them until they were out of sight. The gunfire slowed to an intermittent crackle and then fell silent. Powder-smoke drifted through the encampment still, acrid in the nostrils. Casey reloaded his Colt with his belt shells and finally, almost with regret, holstered it.

'Dad!' It was Marly who had cried out. She crawled from under the wagon, sprang to her feet and rushed across the encampment. Looking that way Casey could see that Jason Landis had been hit, though how badly he could not tell. He started that way at a jog-trot.

A small boy sat lugging a yellow dog with floppy ears next to a wagon wheel. His eyes were bleak. Beyond him Casey saw four or five men, one woman, huddled around the still form of a man. When the woman rose, she turned away, hands to her mouth and rushed off, leaving her shawl behind her as she ran. Moments later a keening sound, a sorrowful wailing could be heard. The young boy hugged his dog more tightly.

'Nicked at least three of them myself,' an angular, dark-eyed man was saying to a group of settlers. Casey had seen only two raiders down against the cold earth, and he knew that he was responsible for at least one of them, but maybe a little braggadocio was necessary to keep up his courage. It made no difference anyway.

What mattered was the sight of Marly in her oversized coat, on her knees, hovering over Jason Landis. Two other people were there when Casey approached. Marly turned haunted eyes toward Casey. 'He's badly wounded,' the girl said.

'It's his leg,' a stout man Casey had never met, told him confidentially. 'Shattered bad.'

'Doc!' someone else called out to a gaunt man with a haunted expression. 'Come over here. It's Landis!'

The man in the threadbare suit – 'Doc' – approached as if against his will. He seemed to be tugging the chains of his memories after him. They let him through to examine Jason Landis whose face was tight with the anguish of pain.

'Can you patch him up?' the stout man enquired eagerly. Doc looked at him as if he were a fool.

'I haven't practiced medicine since the war, Bailey. I have no surgical tools, nor even a medical bag. In the war,' Doc continued, rising from his inspection of Landis's wound, 'we were compelled to perform certain kinds of surgery. Sometimes twenty . . . fifty operations a day. Without morphine or any other deadening substance, I simply used what I had: a sharp saw and four good men to hold the patient down.'

'You won't!' Marly shouted. She had taken off her buffalo coat to place it under her father's head as a pillow. Her eyes were imploring and defiant at once.

'No, young lady,' Doc replied hollowly. 'I won't. It's the reason I quit practicing medicine after Appomattox.' He ran an unsteady hand over his gaunt, gray face. 'Let's splint the leg the best we can and hope Jason can make it to Sundown.'

One younger man sprinted off to try to find laths or similar strips of wood to make a splint. Jason's face was spasming as he tried to contain the pain. His teeth were tightly clenched, his face colorless. There was no more blood in Marly's face. She looked around helplessly from one man to the other. Almost shame-faced, though none of this had been their doing, the settlers began to wander away.

'Wait!' Jason Landis shouted out, his voice surprising in its strength, and the settlers halted in their tracks and turned back toward Landis. The youngster who had gone to find wood for a splint was back and as Doc, muttering to himself, crouched over Jason Landis working on his broken limb, Landis continued to speak through obvious pain.

'What is it, Jason?' a burly man with a two-inch long red heard asked. He had his rifle cradled in the crook of his arm. His small eyes were dark and emotionless.

'Casey Storm is taking over for me,' Landis said, surprising no one so much as Casey.

'Who the hell is—?'

'That's him,' Landis said, pointing out Casey. The other men shifted hostile eyes in Casey's direction.

'We don't even know who he is!' the big man exploded.

'Don't argue with me, Barrow,' Landis said, wincing as Doc tightened a bandage around his shattered leg. 'You all elected me as wagon-master. Obviously I can't fulfill my duties just now, but I figure you gave me the authority to do what must be done. Casey

Storm is my man. He's a soldier. . . .'

Landis gasped and closed his eyes tightly. He seemed on the verge of passing out. He managed to sit up halfway and with his right hand he passed his .50 Sharps rifle to Casey as if he were passing the scepter of command.

'Look, Colonel,' Barrow said, using Landis's military title for the first time, confirming Casey's suspicions. 'I thought we had all agreed that Joe Duggan is second-in-command.'

'He still is,' Landis said, sitting up with a groan. Marly and Doc helped the wagon-master to his feet. 'Now he's second to Storm here. That shouldn't be too difficult to understand.'

'We don't even know this man,' Barrow said, tugging angrily at his growth of red beard. 'Where's he come from? What is he doing here! We'll have to hold a meeting about this, Landis.'

'Hold your meeting, then,' Landis said, balancing unsteadily on one leg. 'But hold it tonight. We have to reach Pocotillo Creek today, and you know that. Let's get these wagons moving and save the bickering until we have time for it.'

'Doc let Casey take his position under Landis's right arm and with Marly on the left they began to make their unsteady way back toward the wagon. They hadn't gone ten yards before a well-built man with a bullish face stormed up to them, his face a mask of fury. On his heels a svelte daisy of a woman with long blonde hair worn loose in the morning trailed after him with the supremely confident bearing of one who knows her beauty and trusts it as free passage through life.

'Hold up there, Landis!' the scowling man called out sharply. 'What's this that Barrow is telling me – that this stranger is taking command of the wagon train?'

Joe Duggan was a long-striding, angry man wide through the shoulders, darkly handsome, and just now in a fury. Jason Landis was unsteady on his feet, his weight bearing down on Casey Storm and that of his small daughter as they paused to await Duggan's arrival.

'I said that,' Landis answered heavily. His chin was nearly resting on his chest. He needed sleep and a lot of it.

'You must be out of your mind!' Duggan bellowed. The blonde girl, far too pretty to be out here on the long Montana plains, moved up beside Duggan, her smile flirting, knowing, deep at once. If a kitten could smile, it would have looked like hers. Duggan placed a proprietary hand on her arm and had it gently, deftly brushed away.

'Barrow is planning a meeting tonight,' Landis said through his obvious pain. 'For now, let's work together to reach the Pocotillo. We haven't had water for our stock for two days, and my horses won't eat snow to survive.'

Duggan wouldn't let it go. 'Who the hell are you?' he demanded of Casey. 'Where'd you pop up from? You could be a McCoy man for all we know. Have you got a horse, a destination?'

'Only of the most nebulous sort,' Casey Storm answered frankly. Duggan looked puzzled by the reply.

'He means "no",' the blonde lady said, with a smile that seemed directed only at Casey Storm.

'I don't like this,' Duggan said, shaking his head. 'I don't like it at all.' He glanced at the sky. 'You're right, though, Landis. We have to keep moving if we're going to reach Pocotillo Creek by nightfall. For now we'll let this slide, but we *will* have that meeting tonight and see how things stand after that.'

'Puny little pup. Insolent to the point of offensiveness,' Landis muttered, as Duggan and the blonde ambled away.

'However, he does have a point, you know,' Casey said, as he and Marly helped Landis back to the covered wagon. 'I don't know you people. I have no idea of the situation. I'm totally unqualified to take command of a group like this.'

'You're qualified,' Landis said, as they helped him up on to the tailgate and from there into the bed that had been Marly's the night before, and covered him with a buffalo robe and three tightly woven, colorful Indian blankets.

'Take charge for me, Casey,' the old man said and

then closed his eyes. Casey felt like a foot-soldier given a battlefield commission, but he also felt more than uncomfortable. He did not want the obligation, the mantle of responsibility. No one in the camp wanted him to assume it. 'You can use my mount of course. . . .' Landis murmured. 'Marly can. . . .'

Then the old soldier could withstand the pain from his wounds and the trials of the morning no longer and he fell into a deep, troubled sleep. Marly and Casey slipped from the wagon and stood watching as the caravan began to trundle its way westward across the slush left behind by the brief snowstorm. It was Casey's first real look at the cavalcade. Six covered wagons with a husband and wife on the bench seats, children peering out from under the canvas, or briefly running alongside with exuberant abandon until they were scolded to clamber aboard. The single yellow dog with its folded ears and feathery tail, tongue lolling happily. Then the business portion of the troupe. Four heavy freight wagons, three of them loaded with stacked sawn lumber, drawn by six-mule teams, their five-foot high wheels churning up the mud and snow in their passing. These were flanked by outriders, the red-bearded Barrow and the dark-eyed Duggan among them. The latter carried a heavy scowl which he fixed on Casey as he trailed past, rifle across his saddlebow.

Behind these rumbling conveyances came a light wagon driven by a thin man so pale as to be almost albino. Beside him sat the blonde woman in a yellow dress and wide yellow bonnet. A long, yellow, sheepskin-lined coat covered her shoulders and legs. She waved a cheerful hand at Casey as they passed.

At Casey's shoulder, Marly said, 'We're last.'

'Looks that way,' Casey agreed. He glanced down at Marly, saw her wide dark eyes lost in consideration, and he asked, 'What is it?'

'I was just wondering if you were in love with her yet'

'In love with. . . ?'

'With Holly,' Marly said, lifting her chin in the direction of the light wagon where the blonde woman rode. 'All of the men fall in love with her. I just wondered if you were yet.'

'At this time, in this temperature,' Casey said, drawing his buffalo coat more lightly around him, 'I haven't given it a thought. Where's your father's horse?'

'He's ground-hitched beside the team. Checkers – that's his name – is saddled and ready. Will you be riding out?' Marly asked with a sort of sad expectation in her voice. Casey glanced again at the tiny, big-eyed girl. The wind shifted her dark, loosely contained hair. What was it she thought? That he would steal Landis's horse and simply ride away? Did she fear being alone so much, or had she had other men just ride away from her? Casey looked at the long Montana plains, streaked with snow-melt, studied the high-blossoming clouds in the pale blue sky. Before he had fallen into this confusion, he had been riding from nowhere, going nowhere. He smiled dimly, trying to comfort the girl as he told the truth to himself.

'Hell, where would I go?'

Casey retrieved the high-shouldered, sturdy Appaloosa gelding – Checkers – from its ground-hitch, carried the iron to the back of the wagon, flung it aboard and tied Checkers with thirty feet of tethering rope to the tailgate.

'Shouldn't you be on the flank?' Marly asked, as he clambered up into the box beside her, fitted his gloves and took the reins. 'That's what Father always does – checking the trail, watching for breakdowns, and for the McCoy men.'

'That's what I should be doing, yes,' Casey said, releasing the brake and snapping the reins to put the mismatched team into motion. 'But I need to know a little more – no, a lot more – about what I've gotten myself into and what sort of hell might lie ahead. I'm riding blind and I don't like it. It's time you told me what this is all about, Marly.'

THREE

The wind from the north was chilling, shifting the horses' manes as it passed. The stacked cumulus clouds, like massive white battlements against the blue sky, cast long cloud shadows in their slow progress over the long prairie where melting snow mirrored the bright sun.

Marly had taken over the driving chores, guiding the team of horses deftly, the reins loose in her gloved hands. Ahead of them the long line of wagons arrowed westward leaving deep muddy ruts behind in their passing. Casey Storm glanced at a slowly circling golden eagle, high aloft, soaring effortlessly on the air currents, and repeated his question.

'What is this all about, Marly? I have to know all of it if I'm going to have any chance of helping you out.'

'Father's the one you should talk to,' Marly said.

'It's going to be a while before I have the chance

to talk to him,' Casey said, glancing into the interior of the wagon where Jason Landis, smothered with blankets, tried to sleep off his pain. 'Let's start simply: where are you people from? Where are you going? Who is McCoy and why is he trying to prevent you from it?'

'*Simply*?' Marly smiled, as if Casey had made a joke. She returned her dark eyes to the broken trail ahead and said apologetically, 'All right. I'll do my best. But this has been going on for so long that it can't be simply explained.'

'Try,' Casey urged. Marly nodded her head resolutely and told him.

'We were all small shareholders on about a thousand acres of land near the Yellowstone. Dirt farmers, I guess you'd call us,' Marly said. 'For most of us it was our first chance to own our own land. We tilled the soil, grew our small crops. It was a rugged life – we lived in soddies and got soaked every winter!' Marly laughed as if she were thinking about a time long past.

'Go on. What happened?' Casey prodded.

'What happened,' Marly said with seriousness, 'was that one day a man named Gervase McCoy sent two United States marshals and about a dozen hired gunmen to our farm. You should be talking to Father about the legal situation . . . but,' she went on, after a moment's hesitation, 'the upshot of it was that through the Bureau of Land Management McCoy had somehow been granted legal title to all of our property and we were given two months to appeal or vacate.'

'So, of course, you did appeal.'

'Of course we did not!' Marly said in a fiery voice. 'It would have required sending a delegation to Denver! The hearing would have taken at least six months and by then our untended farms would have been in ruins through neglect. It was not certain that we would have won anyway. McCoy had the money to hire legal experts. We did not.'

'I see,' Casey commented, although he did not – entirely. The wagon slued across a particularly muddy patch of earth, churned up by the heavier wagons ahead of them. Marly's face which had grown grim now relaxed as the team found its footing and they proceeded more easily onward.

'Where was I?' she asked absently.

'You were telling me about McCoy.'

'Yes. Well, things weren't moving along quickly enough for Gervase McCoy and so he decided to accelerate them. We began to be attacked by night-riders. Crops were trampled, stock driven off, two men were shot from ambush.'

'Why didn't you just pack up and leave then? Since you couldn't win in court and weren't prepared to fight?' Casey asked.

'Why!' Marly laughed again, but there was no humor in it. 'You'd have to understand how things stood. With no crops, virtuality no food – all we had was our root crops, potatoes, parsnips and such – and what meat the hunters managed to bring in. Most of our horses and oxen had been run off by McCoy's men.'

'The Shadow Riders,' Casey interrupted.

'Who?'

'That's what I call them.'

'I see. All right. It suits as well as anything else, I suppose,' Marly said. 'I don't know where they all came from – Joe Duggan says that he believes them to be army deserters. He might be right. I know McCoy can afford to pay them a lot more than the army ever could!'

'You were going to explain—'

'Have you no patience?' Marly said, but she said it lightly. 'When you went to school did you expect to get your education in one day?'

'Actually, I did have hopes,' Casey replied with a rueful grin, reflecting briefly on his unhappy school days.

'Nevertheless,' Marly went on, slowing the team as they reached a muddy dip in the trail, 'Father and a few of the other men – Joe Duggan and Mike Barrow among them – decided that they were fighting a losing war with McCoy, and voted to pool the few resources we had left to purchase new land with an uncontestable claim farther west. Father and Duggan found a large parcel on the Little Missouri not far south of Fort Benton. Father said it was lush with buffalo grass, green and golden as they surveyed it from a knoll at sundown.

'The last owner had been a failed English landholder who had grown tired of the American West and sick of Montana winters and was willing to sell out at almost any price offered. The deal was struck, the town-to-be christened Sundown and our destination was set. We had sixty days to reach Sundown, and that seemed to be plenty of time for us to organize.'

'It all sounds propitious,' Casey commented. 'What went wrong?'

'What?' Marly released another of her humorless laugh. 'Everything that could go wrong. The Englishman, it seems, sold us homestead land, not property that he legally owned.'

'But you have legal title now.'

'Oh, yes! Father was determined that we wouldn't be displaced again. We have legal title – under the Homestead Act. Do you know anything about that?'

'Not much,' Casey admitted.

'It was enacted to prevent people from claiming large tracts of land speculatively. Never intending to live on it, to use it for anything but turning a profit.'

'That much I knew,' Casey said.

'It was intended to help families, hard-working people without a square inch of land to call their own, to settle the wide country.'

Casey cut her short. She was growing too angry again. He touched the tiny woman on the shoulder and she shifted her wide eyes to him, attempting a smile.

'What happened, Marly?'

'Well,' she said with a shrug, followed by a sigh, 'in order to claim land under the Act, it's required that improvements be made, that one can show that the claimants are actually residents there.'

'To prevent the land-grabbers from gobbling up the Territory.'

'Yes, exactly. That is where the second part of our battle began. McCoy now covets Sundown and the surrounding country. I think the man is crazy! He wants to own all of Montana.'

'Someone must have told him what was happening,' Casey said thoughtfully.

'That idea has passed through my mind. And Father's.'

'But you said you had two months to reach the Little Missouri, Marly. Two months to prove-up on the land. Obviously with all these building materials, you all expected to reach Sundown and build some kind of settlement to prove your claim. Why then. . . ?'

'Why then?' she replied with a hint of mockery. 'You got a taste of it last night. I told you that our stock was driven off. To assemble new teams of horses out here we found ourselves compelled to deal with the Lakota Indians. A simple disagreement over language turned into a conflict.

'Joe Duggan said that he had met the Indians' price for their horses, but that they were demanding whiskey and rifles as well which obviously we don't have even if we were inclined to trade them.'

Casey nodded. He watched the mismatched team drawing the wagon, understanding now how they had been roughly assembled, why Marly had difficulty from time to time managing the ponies which they must have tried to break to harness nearly overnight.

'Still . . .' he said.

Marly held up a gloved hand and reminded him, 'I know, you still don't understand – but you weren't there, and I did say you couldn't expect an education in one day.' She smiled weakly. 'Day after day McCoy's snipers harassed us. Our food supplies grew low. The winter began to settle in – you've seen what these snowstorms can be like. We holed up for some time, fearing the Indians who seemed to have found their whiskey somewhere. Mrs Troupe was due to deliver her baby in a few days and her husband, rightly, refused to leave for Sundown, and Troupe is the man who owns the lumber wagons. Oh, Casey,' she said, using his name for the first time that he could remember, 'it was grueling.'

'But now?'

'But now,' Marly answered, 'we have only six days

left to reach the new landholding. If we do not occupy it, prove up on it by then – by law, it falls back into the public domain and I can assure you that though I do not know what legal maneuvers he will use – Gervase McCoy will lay claim to Sundown.'

Casey Storm fell silent. He watched the slow miles pass, the cold sun riding high in a pale sky. The eagle had drifted away and become only a lost harbinger against the lonesome sky. What had he, himself, drifted into? He was no one's savior, but only a rambling man with troubles of his own clinging to him. Why had Jason Landis passed this burden on to him? Casey had nothing to do with these sodbusters' problems, did not wish to inherit them, nor to tangle again with the Shadow Riders.

He wished that he were this Stan Deveraux the settlers had depended upon to aid them. Casey still did not know a thing about Deveraux, although he had a fairly good idea now of who he was, and why they had sent for him. Casey glanced at the wide-eyed girl with the unruly dark hair, her face intent as she guided the team of horses, urging them along the rutted, muddy road to nowhere. To Sundown.

He looked at her and silently cursed himself.

'They're out there,' Casey said in a low voice that barely carried above the clopping of hoofs and the creak of the wagon's axles.

'I know they are,' Marly said, glancing briefly to the north. 'What can you do about it, Casey?'

'I don't know. I'm not Deveraux.'

'No,' she agreed quietly, 'but Deveraux is not here. You are, and Father has assigned you the task.'

Assigned or not, Casey felt that he had an obligation to help the settlers get through to Sundown. To help Marly reach her destination and fulfill her hopes for finding a new home. He had her briefly halt the covered wagon as he climbed down and untethered Checkers. The scabbard on the Appaloosa's saddle was fitted to the Sharps .50 that Jason Landis carried and so Casey socketed it there. Additionally he carried his own reloaded Henry repeater and, of course, his belt-gun. It made more sense to ride out loaded for bear than to meet the wild things unarmed.

Briefly he rode the Appaloosa alongside Marly, studying the broad land. Checkers was frisky and eager, but the horse sensed its rider's unaccustomed mannerisms; perhaps the different weight or use of heels and knees than his true owner. However, it settled in obediently after a mile or so and Casey told Marly, 'I'm going to circle north and then trail behind for a way. I doubt McCoy has given up this easily.'

'All right,' Marly said, her face determined and set. 'Did you have the time to talk to Father?'

'He's still asleep,' Casey said, not mentioning that he had doubts the old man would ever awaken again.

The country had begun to change. Low, folded,

snow-streaked hills lifted from the plains. Pine trees, scattered but impressive in their height, stippled the land. Casey rode away from Marly silently, regretfully. Guiding Checkers up the slope of a low knoll he took the time to simply sit the pony and sweep the distances with his eyes. There was no sign of trailing riders, no sign at all of human habitation. The scent of the pines was rich and deep. A colony of crows raised a racket in the forest. Far to the west Casey could make out the silver-blue ribbon of Pocotillo Creek where they must halt to water their stock. He could make out no trace of the upper Missouri, but even farther to the west he could see the snow-crowned Rocky Mountains, their shadowed flanks deep purple in this light, massively impressive even at this distance.

Casey rode the spotted horse eastward, watching the backtrail. The wagons had begun to diminish in perspective, becoming the size of toys against the vast sweep of the prairie. An incoming rider emerged from the trees and Casey's hand dropped automatically to his holster. The lady drew up her horse.

'Don't shoot! I give up,' Holly Bates said with an impish smile. She drew nearer, her blonde hair loose, her hands light on the reins of her white-stockinged sorrel.

'What in the. . . ! What are you doing out here?' Casey managed to ask with a critical shake of his head.

'They say it's a free country,' Holly answered lightly.

'Hardly the point,' Casey said, more roughly than he intended.

'No,' Holly said, slightly abashed now. 'I might have been looking for you.'

'But you weren't,' Casey countered.

'No,' Holly laughed, brushing back a tendril of pale hair. She now wore a divided riding skirt, blue blouse and heavy black leather jacket. 'I had to get off the wagon – you try riding eight hours a day with Abel.' Casey assumed that she meant the albino who drove her rig. 'He's a mute, you know?'

'No, I didn't.'

'He is. Sometimes it's a blessing, but it doesn't do much to promote conversation.'

'Why did you hire him?' Casey asked.

'I sort of inherited him from my family,' Holly told him. 'Abel isn't capable of holding many jobs. My father took him in years ago out of pity. He's been around since I was a little girl.'

'Holly – a woman riding alone out here – it's totally reckless,' Casey said.

'Isn't it! But then, I'm a reckless sort of woman, Mr Storm.' Holly laughed again. The breeze shifted her light hair. Her eyes blue and merry, so different from Marly's wide dark eyes – reflected amusement and the same proud confidence Casey had noted in her before. She smiled again, pursing her lips prettily and Casey could see what Marly had meant about every man Holly met falling in love with her. It wouldn't have been that difficult. Casey forced a growl into his tone.

'Let's catch up with the wagons. We need to be there when they make camp on the Pocotillo.'

'Oh, yes,' Holly said, again without a hint of seriousness – perhaps she was just one of those people who managed very well making their way frivolously through life. 'That's where they intend to fire you, isn't it?'

Casey's smile was rueful. 'I don't know. If Joe Duggan and Barrow have their way, I suppose so.'

'Don't you care?'

'Not much. So long as someone will let me borrow a pony and loan me some grub.'

'May I ask. . . ?' Holly hesitated. 'Where is it that you are going, Mr Storm?'

They had started their horses down the slope, following in the wake of the wagons. The pine trees began to thin again and they found themselves on the muddy flats. Casey answered eventually, 'It's growing too late in the year for it now, but I always thought that I wanted to cross the Rockies. Once they could be breached, there's a new world to be found. What sort of world, I don't know. Some sort of new world.'

'You're a drifter, then,' Holly said, condensing the rambling explanation Casey had given her.

'Yes,' he admitted. 'Only that.'

'So are we all,' Holly said, with what seemed to be genuine understanding. Their horses had settled into a cadenced, evenly paced walk. 'But tell me, Mr Storm – are you drifting toward something or away from something. Some*one*, perhaps?'

Casey didn't answer. He did not care to revisit Cheyenne in his mind. He smiled faintly and they rode on in companionable silence as the clouds drifted away and the shadows beneath their horses' legs grew longer. He found himself if not loving, then liking Holly Bates. She seemed to intuitively know when not to trespass further into a man's private thoughts, and God knew she was beautiful enough with her pale hair drifting, erect, trim figure sitting easily in the saddle.

Why then was he uneasy?

In the first place it was certain that she had not ridden out looking for him, an excuse she had lightly made. It was equally certain that she had not wandered away from the wagon train, ridden out so far just for a brief respite from Abel's company. There was no reason she couldn't have traveled ahead and had a conversation with some of the women – or men – with the wagons. Riding out here alone was reckless, and the woman knew it. The Shadow Riders were all around them. Killers. Holly was hardly a stupid woman. It made no sense unless there was another, deeper reason behind it.

Like wishing to meet someone else out here. McCoy? One of his men? A secret lover in the enemy camp? Could she be involved with the badmen in some way? Casey could not come up with a logical reason how that could be so. Why?

Then again – damn all! – he had only fallen into this dark web the night before. He did not know his enemies from his friends – assuming he had any of those. By the time they reached the wagon camp on the Pocotillo where the horses were being watered, the fires built under the shelter of the towering jack pines, his temples were pounding with a pain nearly equal to the constant tomrment of his injured ribs.

He wanted desperately to trust someone!

But then again that was what had started all of his troubles back in Cheyenne.

There was no one left to trust.

Marly was there watching as Casey and Holly rode into the sheltered camp and swung down from their ponies. The look in her wide, dark eyes was not judgmental, but only resigned. The tin cup of coffee she might have been saving for Casey turned in her hand and was emptied out on to the ground.

'Uh-oh,' Holly said, 'she's jealous.'

'She doesn't even know me,' Casey Storm grumbled, swinging down to lead Checkers to the Landis wagon.

Whether Marly was or wasn't jealous, there was someone in camp who was. The handsome broad-shouldered Joe Duggan stepped in front of Casey as he tried to pass and put a hand an his shoulder. 'Stay away from my woman.'

'All right,' Casey said agreeably.

'I mean it.' Duggan's voice was menacing.

'I said *all right.*'

'We've voted you out, Storm, as I promised we would. You're not in charge of anything!'

'All right,' Casey said again. He nudged his way past the taller Duggan and went to the rear of the wagon to tether Checkers. Duggan wouldn't leave it alone. As Casey tied a slipknot in the tethering rope and reached for the cinch strap to loosen Checkers' saddle, Duggan slammed the heel of his hand roughly into Casey's shoulder. A crowd was gathering. Casey saw the red-bearded Mike Barrow push his way through the assembled settlers to watch.

'*All right*!' Duggan said tauntingly. His fists were bunched now and he was breathing heavily, bent slightly forward. 'That's all you can say? You don't give a damn about any of this, do you, Storm?'

'Not a lot,' Casey admitted. 'I don't know a single one of you. I was just trying to do what Colonel Landis asked me to do.'

'And you don't give a damn about a lady's reputation – waylaying her on the road!'

Which was what this was really about – Holly.

The old stirrings slowly crept over Casey. He did not wish to fight with guns, knives or fists, but a man can be pushed beyond his limit and Joe Duggan was very close to the limit.

'I would never do anything to damage a lady's reputation,' Casey said sincerely. 'Where I was raised, it is not done. Now if you will leave me to my work?' He raised Checkers's stirrup and reached for the cinch and Joe Duggan blind-sided Casey with all of the fury that had been building up in him, driving a hard-knuckled fist against the side of his head.

Casey went sprawling against the cold mud of the earth and lay there trying to blink the stars out from behind his eyes.

Rising on wobbly legs, Casey removed his gunbelt and smiled at Duggan who seemed not to have expected him to get to his feet again.

'Let's have at it then, Duggan. I don't know why you insist on putting both of us through grief, but if that's the way you want it, let's have at it.'

FOUR

Joe Duggan's smile spread confidently over his handsome dark face. Perhaps he had not expected the fight to go this far, but he showed no signs of backing down. Heavier in the chest and shoulders than Casey Storm, he was confident in his abilities. Duggan backed away three paces and allowed Casey to rise unsteadily to his feet. Then the muscular man assumed a fighting position, knuckled hands raised before his face. Casey guessed, correctly, that Duggan had spent some time in a prize-fighting ring.

'Come on then, saddle tramp!' Duggan challenged, as the crowd of onlookers widened the circle around the two combatants to give them room. Duggan was on his toes, his fists held steady.

'The hell with it,' Casey Storm muttered and he charged the man.

Casey had once known a rough-and-tumble fighter from the Kentucky hills named Charlie Biggs. One day after a scrap in which both men had taken a brief part, Charlie had told Casey his theory of fighting. 'Don't let a man choose his own style of fighting. It's like giving a man his choice of weapons in a duel. He'll naturally choose what he feels he is best at. Most men will want to fight you from an upright position. It lets them get set with their practiced maneuvers. I tell you, Casey, what you do is get on top of them, take them down. There aren't many men who have the skills to fight from flat on their backs!'

As Duggan postured for the crowd in his boxing stance, Casey charged, yelling out one indistinguishable, violent word. His shoulder slammed into Duggan's chest and the bigger man was knocked to the ground. Casey heard the wind go out of Duggan as they hit the earth, Casey mauling the bully. The boxer's arms flailed. Duggan was already beaten in body and spirit although he didn't yet realize it.

Casey was swinging his fists even as Duggan collapsed on to his back, now he managed to get his knees up over Duggan's shoulders, effectively pinning him down. Casey was able to punch away with both hands while Duggan kicked out futilely, trying to free himself. Joe's arms, anviled to the ground, were useless against Casey's onslaught.

Duggan rolled his head from side to side, trying to evade the punches Casey was raining down on him, but that too was useless. One terrific, precisely placed right-hand shot from Casey's fist landed on the hinge of Duggan's jaw and the big man's eyes went vacant. The struggle, even the twitching in Joe Duggan's body ceased, and Casey let him go.

Casey rose shakily, stepped back, ran his fingers through his hair and looked slowly around the circle of settlers. 'There's your new hero,' Casey muttered. He turned away then, holding his battered ribs with his right hand. He caught the woman's eye across the battleground. Holly Bates had been there, watching, and her blue eyes now gleamed with a sort of triumphant pride.

Casey moved weakly toward the Landis wagon. He had had enough of these people. More than enough. One man whom Casey didn't know murmured, 'That didn't hardly seem fair.'

Casey brushed past him and continued to the tailgate of the wagon. Pulling himself up over the tailgate, he sagged to the floor at the foot of Colonel Landis's bed. The old man asked quietly, 'I heard the uproar. What happened, Casey?'

'Nothing. Just a crowd gathered around to watch Joe Duggan beat the hell out of me.'

'Did he?'

Casey didn't answer the exhausted old man. Landis's face was as pale as the canvas of the covered wagon, drawn and haggard. 'I'm pulling out,' Casey replied instead. 'What's the chances of me using Checkers until you can ride again, Colonel?'

'Think you'll ever bring him back?' the colonel

asked. Then he fell into a racking coughing fit.

'I'll try to,' Casey answered sincerely.

'I believe you, son. Thing is, I don't know if I'll ever be able to ride again. Not the way my leg feels now. Fiery. Dead. Changes from moment to moment. I think Doc was only trying to spare Marly's feelings when he said he wouldn't have to take my leg off. Maybe Doc never would – his war experiences weighing so heavily on him – but I think it's going to come to the point where *someone* will have to remove it.'

'All we can do is hope not, sir,' Casey said. His breath had returned and his side did not now ache so abominably. 'About Checkers. . . ?'

'Take him. Be good to him. I love that big Appy,' Landis said from behind closed eyes.

'I hope our paths cross again soon, sir,' Casey said, struggling to his feet.

'You're set on going, then?' Landis asked, his eyelids parting only fractionally.

'I don't care for these people, frankly. And they don't want me here, or need me.'

'What about Marly?' the old soldier asked.

'I don't understand you, sir.'

'Yes you do, Casey.' Landis tried to lift his head, failed and settled back, eyes closed once more. 'I'm all she has, and now I've let her down. I'll likely not even make it through to Sundown.'

'You have years ahead of you,' Casey said with shallow confidence.

'With God's grace, perhaps. But, Casey, right now – the condition I'm in – I can't do anything to protect her! Help her!' he pleaded. 'You're young; you can. At least,' he said weakly, 'to Sundown.'

'The settlers don't want me around.'

'It doesn't matter what they want!' Landis snapped. 'I can't make them accept you as a leader, but I can make them understand that you're my employee and friend – if I may call you that. Find Doc, Art Bailey, Mike Barrow, Virgil Troupe – send them over here. I want to make it clear that you are working for me and I want you around watching out for Marly. At least until Sundown.'

Landis fell silent then. His breathing grew more shallow and began to rattle deep in his chest. Casey turned away slowly, making his way toward the wagon's tailgate.

'At least until Sundown,' Casey promised the old man beneath his breath.

What else was there to do? Leave Marly alone? The old man was right – he was probably dying. McCoy's Shadow Riders were still back there and they would come again. There was no doubt about that. Casey glanced at the shallow, slow-running Pocotillo Creek, blue-violet in the dusky light. The frogs had begun their night-grumbling along the willow-clotted banks of the rill. The last of the clouds had dissipated and the stars formed a brilliant, broad banner across the long Montana skies. The settlers were in their wagons where lanterns gleamed dully, lighting the canvases. A few men here and there sat over low-burning camp-fires drinking coffee and discussing their pasts, the day's events, or future hopes.

Casey looked again to the stars, and then away again, tramping onward. Every last glimmer of light from the sun had broken and fled into the depths of the night.

There were now only five days to Sundown.

She came from out of the darkness of the shifting pine shadows. Casey had never seen her trembling and fearful before, but now Marly was.

'Is Father . . . all right?' she asked, touching his arm. 'I know his wound is terrible.' She raked uncertain fingers through her long dark hair. 'I was just pretending that I did not know how bad it was. Is he . . . alive?' She looked away as she asked that question.

'Yes. He's weak but still with us. I'm sure he'll be all right, Marly,' Casey lied.

'And you?' Marly asked, looking up at him with wide, starlit eyes. 'Are you still with us, Casey? Or will you be going away now?'

Casey smiled thinly in the night. Taking her by her arms, he said, 'I'm staying, Marly. I promise you.'

He felt her body slacken with relief. Briefly her forehead rested against his chest. There was no way of knowing if it was his optimistic words about her father, or his vow to stay with her, that was more responsible for her relief. A mingling of the two, he supposed. He wished at that moment that he could see into the tiny woman's heart. To the depths of it.

And realized that he had never before felt a wish to know a woman that deeply – not really. Briefly he told her what the colonel had requested. There would be far fewer problems if Marly met with the leaders of the wagon train and asked them to visit her father than if Casey himself tried it.

She nodded, turned from him and started on her way. 'Marly?' Casey said in a whisper. The camp was silent, the fires burning low, the stars incredibly, unashamedly bright.

'Yes, Casey?'

'I haven't fallen in love with her.'

Night had settled stiffly, but soon grew brutally cold. There were tiny icicles clinging to the horses' whiskers and the camp-fires had to struggle valiantly to stay alive. The sky was a blanket of diamond stars. Underfoot the muddy earth had grown rime which crackled as a man walked over it.

Casey Storm was walking over it now, his boots breaking the thin ice. Checkers eyed him apprehensively as he approached. The Appaloosa shuddered and side-stepped uneasily as Casey placed his hand on the spotted pony's neck.

'Where are you going, Casey?'

Marly emerged from the night shadows and

walked toward him, a shawl drawn tightly across her shoulders. She had starlight in her eyes and a look of unhappy apprehension as well. She stopped within a foot of Casey Storm and looked up at him, her expression undecided.

'I'm not leaving you,' Casey promised her, as he flipped Checkers' saddle blanket over his back and smoothed it. 'I told you that I wouldn't.'

'I know. I trust you. I believe you,' Marly said, her huge eyes still fixed on his. 'Why then. . . ?' she wondered, as Casey swung the saddle up and over the Appy.

Casey paused in his work. Leaning his shoulder against Checkers, he tilted his hat back and told her in a low voice, 'I'm going to pay McCoy a visit. He has the men, the guns. Far more than we can meet. Things can't go on like this. They'll be hitting us here and there, raiding when they take a notion. The way things are playing out, we won't have a chance of making it to Sundown.'

Marly was suddenly near panic. 'You can't go against him! Not alone, Casey. At least wait until—'

'Until what? Until Deveraux arrives – if he does? That's what he is, a hired gun, right?'

'All the men thought that he would—'

'All the men don't know Deveraux,' Casey said coldly.

'What do you mean? Do *you* know him, Casey?' Marly asked.

'I think so,' Casey Storm said, tightening the cinch of Checkers's saddle. 'If he was summoned from Cheyenne. Yes, I think he's someone I know all too well.'

'Then tell me—'

'Not tonight. Just let it be said that Deveraux and I are hardly friends.'

'All of that is of no consequence,' Marly said, placing a restraining hand on Casey's leg as he swung up into the saddle. 'This is madness! You can't ride off by yourself.'

'And who would go with me?' Casey asked deliberately. 'These men with their wives and children to care for? Joe Duggan or Mike Barrow? There is no one, Marly.'

'I'll ride with you, Mr Storm,' a reedy voice said from out of the darkness. Casey turned sharply in the saddle to see the thin kid he recognized as the man who had raced off to find some wood to splint Colonel Landis's leg.

'What are you doing, hiding out there?' Casey asked roughly. The young man came forward, tugging down his hat determinedly.

'I wasn't hiding. I just happened to be out alone. Heard what you were telling the lady here. My name is Garrett Strong, Mr Storm. I'm nineteen years old. I've been telling everyone all along that we should take the fight to these night riders instead of letting them strike when and where they pleased. No one listened to me. Because of my age, I guess. I don't know. But I would be pleased and honored to ride with you, Mr Storm.'

'Call me Casey, and the answer is "no", Garrett.'

'But I'm more than willing—'

'And apt to get yourself shot. I can't be responsible for that.'

'As you are apt to be shot ... Casey,' the kid replied earnestly.

'I'm only responsible for myself,' Casey told him.

'As I am!' Garrett said fiercely. 'I know what's right and what needs to be done. I'm alone, sir. No one will grieve for me if the worst happens. I want to ride with you.'

Casey studied the earnest blond-headed kid's face carefully. He saw the stubborn insistence there and in his body's posture. He said with gruff reluctance: 'Saddle your pony, Garrett.'

'You shouldn't have done that,' Marly said, as the young man dashed away.

'I know it.'

'He could be killed. You'll only feel guilty if it does happen. It was a big mistake.'

'Marly,' Casey said, before he turned Checkers away, 'I've made nothing but mistakes up to now. What's one more? I won't deny the kid his manhood.'

'This is a sort of insanity!' she insisted, not loudly but with a deep bitterness. 'You may get this young man killed. You may get yourself killed, Casey – for people you don't even care about! For people who care nothing about you.'

'Could happen, I suppose,' Casey said from Checkers's back. 'But Marly – listen to me – this is a question of tactics. Ask your father. We can't simply roll along day after day waiting to be picked off one by one. Men, women, even children. The colonel would agree with me, I think.'

'If he could now understand or agree!' Marly said, looking up at the mounted man. 'You see where his knowledge of tactics has gotten him, Casey.'

'I can't see any other choice, Marly.'

'Then ride away! If that's what you must do,' Marly said, spinning from him to walk away into the shadowy forest. The feeling that Casey had presumed earlier returned now. Someone, sometime had once ridden away never to return to Marly, deserting her heart.

One day, perhaps, he would ask her about it.

Perhaps one day she would tell him.

'I'm ready, Casey,' Garrett Strong said, walking his undistinguished bay horse forward to flank Casey Storm.

Casey's eyes remained fixed on the dark chambers of the night where Marly had disappeared. Then he nodded and said, 'Let's have at it, then.'

They trailed out in the dark of night. There was a spatter of stars against the sky, but the moon was still only a promise hidden behind the bulk of the Rocky Mountains, and Casey and Garrett rode easily, carefully toward their uncertain destination. The tall pines added to the mystery of the night, shadowing the riders at scattered intervals. The old trees swayed heavily in the night breeze. Pine cones dropped to the dark earth where still, here and there, beneath the sheltering trees, snow lingered. The horses' hoofs made almost no sound against the sodden, pine-needle-littered earth.

When they spoke it was in whispers, but the whispering was the loudest sound across the long, empty land.

'What's the plan, then?' Garret Strong asked. His youthful face was eager, excited and yet fearful.

'Plan?' Casey answered with a shadow of regret. 'I have none, Garrett. I just mean to teach the McCoy men that we still have some teeth and that continuing with their raiding will have some consequences.'

'I see,' Garrett said, the unhappiness in his voice obvious as the two horses plodded on.

'Look, Garrett,' Casey said sternly, 'I didn't invite you along. You volunteered. If you don't like the situation, you're free to return to the wagon camp. No shame attached.'

'It's not that, Casey!' the kid said emphatically. 'It's just that I wish some of the other men were riding with us. To kind of even things up, you know? I wish that Stan Deveraux had showed up when he was scheduled to. It would have made things easier, that's all.'

'You don't know Stan Deveraux, do you?' Casey asked, his eyes hidden by the shadow of his hat brim.

'No! I just know what people say, Casey. I know that Joe Duggan and Mike Barrow believed in him enough to ante up two hundred dollars to hire him.'

'I see,' Casey said quietly. His mind was going in a dozen different directions now. Two hundred dollars. And what would Gervase McCoy be willing to offer the Cheyenne gunman to switch sides if he were apprised of the situation? Much more, Casey suspected. And why was it that Duggan and Barrow alone had expended the money to hire the gunman and not the entire wagon train?

And just where was the known killer now?

'You talk like you do know Deveraux,' Garrett Strong said, after another half-mile had passed and they had come close to the verge of the forest. The moon was heaving itself above the vast bulk of the Rockies now. The moon shadows were long beneath their ponies, the land deep in darkness in the gullies.

'I know Deveraux,' Casey Storm answered. 'Though that's not what he called himself in Cheyenne. One supposes he has a long, long list of aliases. It keeps the law puzzled. When I met him, he was calling himself Tad Chaney—'

'Wait a minute, Casey. Are you positive this is the same man?'

'I can't be until I see his face.'

Ahead now, gleaming dully in the night they could see three or four camp-fires burning. They could not be absolutely sure that these were in the Shadow Riders' camp, but the odds were good. There were few people traversing this sparsely populated land. They continued on.

'How did you come to know this Chaney – or Deveraux, if that's who it is?' Garrett wondered.

'How? He shot me down in the night, Garrett.' Unconsciously, Casey touched the front of his chest where Deveraux's bullet had exited just below his collarbone, inches from his heart.

'In a fair fight?' the kid asked.

'Everyone said so.'

'Do you mind if I ask what it was over, Casey?'

'Just a woman,' Casey said without bitterness. 'Isn't there always a woman involved?'

'He got you from behind, didn't he?' Garrett asked. Casey nodded.

'He did. I was turning toward him at his call. He got off his shot first. No matter – facing him down in broad daylight would have brought the same result. Deveraux – Tad Chaney – is very, very good with a handgun.'

'Did you go back to brace him?' Gaffed asked, apparently excited by the tale. 'When you healed up, I mean?'

'No, I did not,' Casey said tolerantly. 'The lady had

proved she wasn't worth fighting over. I wasn't going to die for her faded honor, or for my own.'

'Oh,' Garrett Strong said, as if he were disappointed in his new-found hero and had expected a different ending to the story. 'You just rode out of Cheyenne.'

'I just rode out, and here you find me,' Casey said quietly. 'Let's rein up a minute and decide what we mean to do to spook this gang.'

Swinging down from their horses, they crouched together, holding the reins to their horses. By the light of the rising moon, Casey could see that Garrett's face was strained, his eyes indecisive. 'You can still go back,' Casey said gently.

'No.' Garrett's voice was weak, but his tone was firm. 'I won't leave you now. Besides, what's the point in it anyway? Should we wait around for another night like last night and let them shoot us in our beds? It's better to take the fight to them – as you say, to show them that we have some teeth.'

That was what Casey had said and he meant it. The truth was that he, himself, would have preferred to just keep riding away from these people and their problems. But he had made a promise to an old man and his big-eyed daughter.

Casey was tall and narrow, well built under his shirt, but he wasn't the kind of man whose appearance cleared out a bar room when he entered. He had been in his share of fist fights, won some and lost a few. It had been proved to him that he was not a gunman in any real sense. What he was was dogged. When someone had first applied that word to him, Casey had frowned, not knowing if he should take offense or not. The man had explained his meaning.

'What I mean, Casey, is that once you take a notion to do something, you wade in, latch on and see it through to the bitter end. Even when it's not in your best interests! There's just no quit in you, Casey Storm.'

And he wasn't about to quit now.

FIVE

'My father was a Kansas Raider,' Garrett Strong was saying in a low voice as the two sat hunched down, watching the firelight from the camp-fires of McCoy's men. Casey nodded. The tales of Bloody Kansas were known far and wide. 'It's why I'm alone now,' the blond kid went on. 'They hanged him.'

'Sorry,' was all Casey could think to say.

'Doesn't matter now – I barely remember him. He might have deserved it for all I know. But I do remember as a little squirt sitting around the hearth, listening to some of his stories. At that age, it all sounds exciting whether they're embellished tales or not.'

'Sure.'

'What I'm working around to, Casey, is that one of those stories concerned the time Dad and only six other men cut off from Quantrill's main force came upon about two hundred regular Union Army soldiers camped not far out of Lawrence. They were far too few to take on the army, but knew they had to delay them until Quantrill's group had re-formed. Dad and the others decided to strike anyway, in guerilla fashion, hoping to slow the army down.'

'What'd they do?' Casey asked, now interested.

'True or not – I learned later to take my father's story with a grain of salt – they bundled together clumps of brush, soaked them in coal oil and charged the Union camp drawing the burning faggots behind them. Six wagons caught fire, the horses stampeded and the soldiers were caught too much by surprise to do much but wing a few wild shots after them. It sure slowed that unit down, what with chasing down their ponies and all.' Garrett paused.

'What do you think, Casey?'

'I think it's better than anything I had in mind,' Casey admitted. 'Whether it will work or not is a different story. If it does,' he grinned as he rose to his feet, 'you'll have a tale to tell your own son some day.'

They lacked the ingredients that the Kansas raiders had had – coal oil most importantly – but by scavenging among the pines they were able to find plenty of fallen twigs. The entire day had been bright and comparatively warm and these were dry despite the previous night's snow. Additionally, there were stacks of dry pine-needles beneath the scattered trees where the snow had never fallen. They made for excellent tinder.

'This seemed like a good idea at the time,' Garrett Strong said uneasily, as they used their lassos to tie loops around the bundles of wood.

'Might be, might not be,' Casey said as he finished a knot and tied the free end of his lariat in a slipknot around Checkers's saddle pommel. 'It's no time to start second-guessing yourself, Garrett. Can't back away for fear of failing. We try. If it doesn't work, it will hardly be the first battle plan to fail.

'Where's your long gun?' Casey asked, noticing the empty scabbard on Garrett's saddle gear.

'Sold my Winchester to buy my passage West,' the kid said, shame-faced.

'They charged you, did they? That figures, I suppose. Here!' He handed the younger man Jason Landis's .50 caliber buffalo gun and a handful of loose cartridges. 'You might need it. I've got my Henry repeater.'

'What now?' Garrett asked, as he swung into the saddle of his bay horse. 'When do we strike fire to the wood?'

'Let's get a little closer. Say fifty yards from their camp.'

'As soon as they see the flames, they'll start shooting,' Garrett Strong said.

Casey answered grittily, 'As soon as they open fire, *we* start shooting.'

Casey was not too crazy about the plan himself, but

there was a certain sort of logic to it. Men rolled up peacefully in their beds after a long day's ride, horses tethered near at hand, bellies full, warm fires to comfort them set upon by an unknown number of vandals stampeding through their camp, fire flaming in their wake. Bedding set afire, horses driven off in panic, guns unleashed in their direction in the dead of night. The chuck wagon – for there must be one on a drive this long – blazing, foodstuffs and whatever other belongings were stored there, destroyed.

Yes, that would give them pause for thought.

And make them mad as hell.

No matter – the McCoy riders were already determined to gun down the settlers to prevent them from ever reaching Sundown. The lives of women and children, they had proved, meant nothing to them either. Let them be mad, good and mad.

Now as Casey and Garrett Strong neared the camp – so closely that they could hear someone saying something in a boisterous voice – Earl? – they swung down and struck fire to the light kindling, watching the flames catch and flare up brightly. No one in the camp of the Shadow Riders seemed to have noticed the twin blazes as Casey and Garrett Strong remounted. Casey glanced at the uneasy blond youth and nodded. Now was the time to find out how much of Garrett's father's tale had been exaggerated.

The raid could have lasted no longer than thirty seconds.

The Shadow Riders had apparently taken no notice as Garrett and Casey Storm struck fire to their faggots. Perhaps they mistook them for other, distant camp-fires. More likely they were all asleep or nearly so, Morpheus assisted by the addition of hard liquor. When Casey hit the camp, towing his bonfire behind him, he encountered no gunfire. Checkers leaped over two men rolled up in their beds, avoiding them with his hoofs as is the breed's natural instinct. Someone raised an angry challenge, but Casey didn't look away. Horses tossed their heads, broke their tethers and stampeded across the plains in fright.

There was a chuck wagon or supply wagon directly in his path and he swung Checkers into a circle around it, tying a loose knot around the canvas-covered wagon with his lariat. The bundle of fire he dragged behind him followed the revolution and sent up angry golden sparks and tongues of red flame which streaked up the side of the wagon. A man leaped from the covered wagon's shelter, yelling incoherently as the canvas caught fire. Without water available to fight the fire, McCoy's men would be able to do nothing but stand and watch their supplies burn.

Now a few of the Shadow Riders had climbed groggily to their feet and begun firing. But they had only moon-silhouetted figures to aim at, and their firing was sporadic and misdirected. Casey heard a man yowl with pain as one of his own comrade's bullets tagged him in the night-tangled mêlée.

Casey could not see Garrett in the darkness. He untied the slipknot of his lariat, let it fall free and drew his own revolver, sending enough shots back through the darkened camp to send the raiders scattering. Then he spurred Checkers on, racing away from the fire-streaked nightmare.

By chance, as life's most important elements always seem to intrude on a man's well-planned life, a rifle bullet surely fired by luck and not by a skilled marksman, caught Casey low in his back.

The bullet ripped through muscle and ticked off a bone, laying a searing seam, hotter than a branding iron across his body just above the waist. Casey gripped his saddle horn with fearful strength and rode on across the dark Montana plains with desperate urgency. Behind him the Shadow Riders would have recovered their composure, angrily begun to gather what ponies they could, and have taken a vow to track down the men who had done them injury.

Casey rode on, reeling in the saddle. His course was indefinite and meandering. He did not wish to lead his trackers back toward the wagon train. Let the hornets' nest he had swatted have its vengeance directed only at him. He, after all, had no wife or child, was not trying to carve out a new life in the West. He was only a lonesome drifter, going nowhere, the world would not remember or even note his passing.

The pain in Casey's side increased with each mile he rode. Somewhere near midnight – judging by the stars and the moon – it became intolerable. Bright flashes of color sparked in his skull. Nausea heaved against his belly. There were brief episodes of blackness when he had to struggle to remind himself where he was, to cling to the pommel and hold on for dear life.

Then, finally, there came a sea of darkness against which he had no defense, and all of the world spun away into a deep void as he tumbled from the saddle to lie against the cold earth, unable to move or have any hope of fighting off the Shadow Riders when they came. Casey closed his eyes and found that he could not open them again. That, too, was all right. It was peaceful in the grave.

It was snowing again. Casey could see the snow falling when he opened his eyes, but he could not feel it. Instead, improbably, he was warm. Moving his fingers he discovered that a bearskin robe had been thrown over him, and that light from a low-burning fire was flickering across the smoky room he found himself in. How could this be?

He tried to sit up, failed as a surge of pain shot through his side once more, lay back and stared at the ceiling of what he now recognized as a small cave. How had he gotten here? His hand automatically dropped to his holster, found the comfortable walnut grip of his Colt revolver. They had not disarmed him then, whoever they were.

'He opened his eyes,' Casey heard an unfamiliar voice say. 'Bring him some of that sycamore bark tea, Mary. You might twinkle it with a little whiskey.'

'Ya, so,' a second voice answered, this one that of a woman.

Casey managed to lift his head enough to see the man standing near him. An old time plainsman by his dress, wearing buckskins and a curious round raccoon-skin hat with two feathers from a red-tailed hawk thrust into it. Across the cave, crouched near the fire was a woman, neither young nor old, neither stout nor thin, dressed like the Sioux woman she was. Her face was pleasant, bland.

'I think you'll make it,' was the first thing the hatchet-nosed plainsman said, as he crouched beside Casey Storm. 'My wife here swabbed out your wound with boiling water and tied on a poultice of moss and mistletoe berries. Best medicine in the world! Moss clots; mistletoe heals.'

'I thank you,' Casey managed to say through feverish lips.

'No need to. A man does what he can to help another out here. Thank you,' the old-timer said, as his Indian wife came to the bed with a cup of pinkish sycamore-bark tea laced with raw whiskey which the plainsman gave to Casey to sip.

Beyond the mouth of the cave snow still fell,

puzzling Casey. The skies had been clear when he was wounded. 'What day is it?' he enquired weakly, drinking another mouthful of the laced herbal tea.

'Not much need of a calendar out here, but I'd say it's Tuesday by dead reckoning,' the plainsman said. 'Why?'

Three days to Sundown.

'I seem to have lost a few days,' Casey answered.

'Yes. You were out cold for two days and nights. We were wondering at first if you were going to make it, but your fever suddenly broke this morning. You'll make it with a little rest and nourishment.'

'How did I get here? Can you tell me your names? What happened?'

'I'm Deacon Lowe,' the older man said, 'to take the easiest question first, and this is my wife, Mary. Not the name she was born with, but I doubt you could pronounce her Indian name. We happened to be out and about scavenging for what we could find – herbs and such, small game to live on. Come night-fall we came across the camp of the McCoy men and backed away.'

'You know McCoy?' Casey asked.

'All too well,' Deacon Lowe said, glancing at his wife.

'Ya, one man I kee with shover him,' Mary said angrily.

'What did she say?' Casey asked Deacon Lowe, his head still fuzzy.

'Well, son, you understand how it is out here.' Deacon sighed. 'Whites don't like me married to Mary here, Indians don't like her being married to me. As a result, we've kind of separated ourselves from the rest of the world. . . .'

A brief, rapid interchange between husband and wife in a combination of French, English and Mandan that Casey could not follow ensued. He looked expectantly at Deacon when they had finished.

'She wants me to tell the story so that you'll understand why she did what she did. You see, we decided to settle down after our vagabond years – roaming is the way of her people. It was my way as well. We started a little farm. No title to the land, no boundaries. Neither Mary nor I were raised in a society where these things were issues. That is, a man and his woman are settled on a piece of land, it belongs to them – move on and find your own.'

'McCoy wanted it for himself,' Casey guessed.

Deacon nodded soberly. 'Why, I don't know, but he did.' The plainsman went on, 'I was out trying to stock up our meat larder for the winter, hoping to bring in a few elk when McCoy decided to send one of his gunnies out to our little place to try to intimidate Mary . . . and worse.'

'I don't understand you,' Casey said, now growing drowsy from the lack of blood combined with the swallows of frontier whiskey.

'As I said,' Deacon continued, 'an Indian woman out here is not considered a proper match for a white man in marriage, but as for the rest . . . they're generally considered fair game.' Deacon wiped a hint of moisture from his eye. 'I was away hunting, and Mary was working in our little garden when the horseman approached her. He tried to scare her off, and then attacked her, and then. . . .'

'I kee him with a shover!' Mary said, clenching her hands. Casey began to understand.

'Do you have any idea what damage the business end of a round-point shovel can do when it's thrust into a man's belly?' Deacon asked softly. 'From then on we've been on the run from McCoy's men. So when we saw someone racing through McCoy's camp like demons from Hades we could only cheer you on. When we saw that you were hit, we naturally brought you here to patch you up if we could.'

'How about my friend?' Casey asked weakly, his eyes closing again.

'We didn't see another man. If he didn't make it out unscathed, then I guess you could say he gave up his life for a good cause.'

'Garrett's a good kid,' Casey murmured.

'He must be,' Deacon Lowe said, tugging Casey's robe back over him. 'Get some rest now.'

'My horse. . . ?' Casey's voice was barely audible.

'The Appy's fine, we've got him staked out with our own ponies.'

The firelight continued to glow dully. The snow continued to fall beyond the mouth of the cave. Casey fell off once again into a deep, somewhat less troubled sleep.

There was no one there when Casey awoke. An odd sound had awakened him, iron striking stone. Peering into the darkness of the dawn-lit cave he saw the source of the sound. Checkers, tethered loosely to a boulder that had fallen from the roof of the cave, was stamping his feet impatiently. There was no sign of Deacon Lowe and Mary.

They had obviously left to continue their vagabond ways. What else could they have done? Take him with them to slow their travel on their trek toward their destination, whatever it might be? Sitting up with his head aching, Casey saw that they had left a few things behind for him. A waterskin and a small bag of provisions – jerky, parched corn and some small roasted Indian potatoes. Gratefully, he made his breakfast from these.

Casey found his saddle, blanket and bridle placed neatly in a corner of the low-roofed cave and got to work. With his side aching, his ribs still sore, it was not a simple task to saddle Checkers, but it had to be done. Rolling up the bearskin, he tied it behind the saddle with piggin strings.

When he led the Appaloosa from the confines of the cave it was still snowing. Swirling, obscuring skirts of snow, not heavy, but constant, and promising to be long-lasting, twisted down, blurring the land to near invisibility.

Which made his slow exodus safer – no man could see him through the screen of the snowstorm, but also brought with it a nearly insurmountable problem: how was he now supposed to be able to find the wagon train again? No landmarks were evident, and might have been of little help, since he did not know the country that well. Nothing was visible through falling veils of snow except the occasion dark trunks of the scattered pines he passed.

His only hope was to once again find Pocotillo Creek where he had left the wagon train, cross it and continue in the general direction of Sundown. He was traveling slowly, but the lumbering wagons would be moving even slower – assuming they had not halted to try to wait out the storm. No, he reflected, they could not do that. They could not afford to miss their deadline. All of their hopes for a new future would be lost if they could not reach the new landhold on schedule.

Casey rode on through the snow-caused darkness of the day, once again using the constant north wind as his rough compass. His new wound burned with an intensely hot fury despite the freezing chill of the storm. Checkers moved without eagerness, but with a certain stolidness. The Appy, too, was dogged in his approach to the present dilemma.

No sun, no moon, no hint as to his direction guided him through the flurrying snowfall. The wind grew heavier, more intense and the depths of the storm he rode through now grew more darkly obscured.

When the ghostly rider rushed down upon him, his rifle fire brilliant against the shadowed tangle of the storm-blanketed day, Casey shot him dead.

SIX

How the Shadow Rider had found him, Casey could not guess. He could only suppose that it was sheer chance. Perhaps the man himself had been lost in the swirl of the falling snow and gotten separated from his comrades. The muzzle of his rifle had flared out against the darkness, spewing a red-orange dagger of flame in Casey's direction. Casey had drawn his Colt, and not quickly but quite deliberately shot the gunhand down as he charged out of the confusion of the day.

The raider took the bullet high in the chest and his surprised eyes went cold as he tumbled from the saddle of his paint pony, dead even before he hit the ground. Weak, cold and slightly dazed, Casey holstered his revolver and swung heavily from the saddle, his movements infinitely cautious – he could not afford to tear open his side again just as it was beginning to heal.

With a shadow of regret, Casey approached the dead man, now face down in the snow, understanding that the raider, too – whoever he had been – somewhere had friends and family, perhaps a wife, son or daughter to whom he would never return.

The rifle that Casey found beside the fallen, furclad warrior, the one he had used to fire at Casey, swept away all of those compassionate reflections. The man he had shot was no soldier, no warrior for a cause. He was nothing but a cold-blooded murderer.

The rifle was the .50 caliber Sharps that Casey had loaned to Garrett Strong.

Gritting his teeth, Casey picked up the buffalo gun, swung heavily back into the saddle and started once more on his way without a backward glance at the raider who was now being slowly covered by the constant, soft fall of the snow.

Checkers seemed well aware of the landmark ahead long before Casey saw it. The Appaloosa lifted his head energetically, tugged at the reins with a toss of his neck and hastened his pace as Casey guided it through the grove of oaks to where they came upon Pocotillo Creek once more. There was no way of determining if he was upstream or down from where the wagon train must have crossed, but at least Casey now had a general idea of his direction, and glancing at the sky, it seemed actually to be lightening. Perhaps the storm would break.

For now he let Checkers drink from the creek although he remained mounted. Casey did not wish to tempt fate by dismounting and mounting unless it was absolutely necessary. His wound was still in the early stages of healing. And, he still had some water left in the skin that Deacon and Mary had provided. Some day, if possible, he would find the old man and his Sioux wife again and let them know how deeply he appreciated their gifts.

He decided to travel west, only west in hopes of crossing the wagon train's trail again. He rode the reluctant pony across the icy creek as the snow continued to fall, obscuring all. It did seem lighter now, but perhaps that was only wishful thinking. Still the land was deeply shrouded, and now the cold began to smother the heat of Casey's body, seeming to slow the flow of his warming blood. If he could reach the Little Missouri . . . then what? He was not thinking clearly and knew it. How far was the river? Which way would he turn then? North or south? Assuming he even recognized the river, did not mistake it for another, the Marias River for example. He did not know this country, and under these conditions he was riding not only visually blind but unguided by experience.

There was an army post, Fort Benton, the settlers had told him, near the junction of the Marias and the Upper Missouri Rivers. Therefore, logic indicated that if he should strike either of the rivers he could follow it upstream and eventually reach Benton even if he could not again catch up with the wagon train.

Assuming he could last through the bitter night.

Casey kept his head bowed to the brunt of the cold north wind. His mind, though seemingly as bruised as his body, continued to sort through the facts as he knew them, coming to only vague conclusions which presented even more questions. If Fort Benton was as near to Sundown as he had been told, why had not someone among the settlers ridden to the army post seeking protection? No one had mentioned a word about this apparently obvious strategy.

Why, exactly, was Gervase McCoy so intent on destroying these people's hopes for a new life? Could he be that land-greedy when he already owned thousands upon thousands of acres? Yet he had taken his own money, hired this band of killers, the Shadow Riders, when he seemed to have no real need to own Sundown. Casey had been told that Joe Duggan suspected that the riders were army deserters. How could Duggan know that? Could the troops have deserted from Fort Benton?

It was a real possibility, of course. To live out on these lonesome plains without any of the amenities of civilization, under the constant threat of Indian attacks – although these had greatly diminished in the past few years – was not the life most men would choose. And, of course, many of the troopers had not chosen the life for themselves. It was common practice in those times for judges wishing to rid their bailiwicks of malcontents and troublemakers to offer them the choice of a prison sentence or a hitch in the army. The plains were rife with army deserters.

Casey's head was spinning – more from confusion than from the blood he had lost and the trials of the night ride.

'I suppose it's what I deserve,' he thought. 'Getting mixed up in people's affairs, uninvited, without any real understanding of the situation.'

He rode on doggedly, angry with himself, tired of the mad chase, knowing all the time just why he was doing it. He rode with the image of the big-eyed little girl, Marly Landis, if not in the forefront of his mind, at least lingering like a haunting memory that could not be banished.

He had promised her that he would not ride away, and he meant to keep that vow!

Sometime after midnight the snow began to ease noticeably. Once Casey thought he caught the glow of the moon through the hazy curtain of the clouds, and after another hour, with Checkers showing his exhaustion, the first star showed itself, blinking on through the filmy haze of the dying storm. The snow was a foot deep under the hoofs of the weary Appaloosa, and the wind still had a biting edge to it, but he believed now he could survive the night, that hope lay somewhere across the long land ahead of them. The run-down soddy, when it appeared out of the darkness, was a welcome sight. The shanty, with half of its roof fallen in was some sort of shelter. Checkers could go on no longer on this night; that much was obvious by his halting gait. Casey was not sure that he could go farther himself as much as he would have wished it.

The night was windless now, silver-cold as he tramped across the snow beneath the stars and light of the half-moon. He held both of his rifles in his hands, eyed the sod house and entered it. This once had been someone's hope for a new life on the far prairie; now fallen into disrepair as someone's hopes must have done. The floor inside, where the roof had failed was frozen mud and snow, but in a far corner where nature had not yet completely savaged the structure, he found a dry corner, and after leading Checkers inside, Casey curled up beneath his bearskin robe and slept the night away in relative comfort.

Morning sunlight through the gap in the fallen roof was so bright as to be nearly startling when Casey awoke. By the angle of the sun he knew that it was still early and, as he sat up stiffly, rubbing his head, he reached for the bag containing what remained of the provisions Deacon and Mary had left for him. He was faring better on this morning than Checkers. There seemed little hope of finding graze for the horse though perhaps the northern-bred Appaloosa was clever enough to paw away the snow and find some poor forage.

Standing in the doorway of the tumble-down shanty, Casey could look over the brilliant snowfield and guess that the thicker fall would stick to the ground this time. The scattered pines stood lonely sentinel across the land. A featureless, barren sycamore tree formed a stark, corrupt shadow against the pale sky. There was still some color along the line of the eastern horizon, but it was time to be moving on.

Only two days remained to reach Sundown.

With difficulty he managed to saddle Checkers and lead him out into the brilliant glare of the morning. Carefully he searched the wide land with his eyes, seeing nothing of the wagon train, seeing nothing of the McCoy men. As he rode on it struck him as odd that he had not crossed any new hoofprints in the snow if the Shadow Riders were still in pursuit. Unless Casey himself was well off their course – and he did not now believe he was – there should have been some sign of the McCoy men.

Unless McCoy already knew exactly where the wagons were headed and he did not need to pursue them, had just been following a pattern of harassment. Casey shook his head heavily. There was no one to confer with, someone who might be able to enlighten him.

How could McCoy know about Sundown? Why should he care?

Casey guided the Appaloosa through another stand of more closely growing pine trees atop a low knoll and found – miraculously – a small patch of lightly snow-covered grass and let Checkers do his best with it as he swung down to survey the land once more.

He still could not make out the Upper Missouri or the Marias, any sign of human habitation. Nor could he discern the wagon train or any pursuing riders. Nor Fort Benton! Nothing but the long snowy plains and the distant upthrust of the Rocky Mountains. Feeling totally lost, he wandered back to stand beside the unhappy Checkers who continued to try to feed himself with the poor, frozen graze.

McCoy knew where the wagons were going. He felt sure of that.

Casey tried to think back to the smattering of information he had been given. Hadn't Marly said something like, 'Father and Joe Duggan found a parcel of land on the Upper Missouri'. Then Duggan could have passed the information on to McCoy. But why would he? Casey rubbed his forehead with the heel of his hand. Maybe he had conjured up that suspicion just because he personally disliked Duggan. Was it possible that Duggan had been working for McCoy all along? Casey rubbed his head once more as if that could stimulate thought. What if

McCoy had instructed Duggan to lead the colonel to Sundown and convince him that this was the spot for the settlers?

None of it fitted, and yet it *did* in a jumbled sort of way.

'Joe Duggan thinks that the raiders are army deserters.' Marly had told Casey. What would have given Duggan that idea?

Duggan along with Mike Barrow had been insistent on driving Casey away from the wagon train so that Duggan could take charge once Jason Landis had been shot. Was it really a Shadow Rider's bullet that had hit Landis during the furious fight, or had someone used the battle as a screen to try murdering the colonel?

And just who in hell had suggesting hiring Deveraux, whom Casey Storm suspected was the Cheyenne gunfighter, Tad Chaney? Garrett Strong had told him that Mike Barrow and Joe Duggan had anted up the money to hire the notorious killer between themselves.

As far as that went, where had Deveraux got to? Casey supposed that the gunman could have just taken the money and run off with it, but men in Deveraux's profession had to keep their bargains if they were to continue to be hired.

'Horse,' Casey said wearily, as he remounted Checkers, 'I can't make sense out of any of this. All I know is that something is very rotten here.'

Checkers did not care enough to twitch an ear to listen. Checkers was as weary as Casey Storm and much hungrier. They continued their westward ride.

An hour along the trail they found the dead man.

One of his arms was outstretched, his body curled up tightly, face hidden by snow. Checkers chuffed and backed away unhappily. At first Casey supposed he had discovered the final resting place of Garrett Strong, but as he swung down wearily and approached the dead man he found that it was not Garrett.

The man was youngish-old. His features, pale and now drawn down in rictus, were those of a person of thirty or so, but his frozen beard was gray.

Casey knew him.

It was Virgil Troupe, the man whom he had met only briefly with the wagon train; he who owned the freight wagons that carried the sawn timber for the new town of Sundown. He who had delayed the start of the settlers' trek westward because his wife had been in the labor of childbirth. A man looking to build a new life with a young wife and a newborn child now destined to spend eternity sprawled on the frozen plains, subject to the cruel use of the scavengers.

Casey rose, cursed silently and looked around. There were no traces of wagon-wheel ruts, none of passing horses. Virgil Troupe, then, had been killed before or as the snow fell. However grimly, the body did mark the trail for Casey. He had no implements for the task of burying Troupe, and the ground – had he any tools – was frozen. Nothing could be done. A quick search of the body produced nothing that might give aid or comfort to Troupe's widow.

The brief investigation did provide two intriguing, quite disturbing bits of information: Troupe's revolver, a Remington .36, was still holstered, fully loaded. And the single shot that had killed the freighter was to the back of his skull. The man had been taken by surprise without a struggle and executed at close range.

That made it very unlikely to Casey that this was the work of the Shadow Riders.

It was someone connected with the wagon train who had done it, had to be.

Weary to the point of emptiness, Casey swung back into the saddle and continued his lonesome trek.

The rising sun warmed his back and glittered off the fallen snow, but the warmth did not reach his bones or stir the chilled blood in his veins. He wished more than once that he had never fallen into this confused, melancholy situation. Had he never met the Shadow Riders he might have passed all of this trouble by now and made his way into Idaho. There were even moments, now, that he considered turning his back on the tangled, unfathomable situation and leaving the strangers to their own problems. And he might well have.

Except for the promises he had made.

Sullenly, Casey made his way westward, the weary pony slogging its way through the snow. At noon, or near to it, Casey picked out the silver-blue glint of running water through the pines. He took it for the Upper Missouri River, or the Little Missouri as it was also called, and his eyes, heart and energies all seemed to come back into focus. Oddly, Checkers's lethargy also seemed to lift and, as they made their way down out of the low foothills, their spirits were higher.

They came along the lone rider in the shadowed valley.

A man completely unfamiliar to Casey Storm was riding parallel to the river, leading a pack horse which seemed well provided with provisions for long-riding. He hailed Casey first, lifting a leather-clad arm in greeting. Hesitantly Casey approached the man, wary of yet another ambush. The Montana country had not been kind to him thus far. He continued forward slowly, his Henry repeater across the withers of his horse, glancing north and south, east and west for other concealed men. There seemed to be none, so Casey angled Checkers up beside the man on the sorrel, cautious but curious.

'Is your name McCoy?' the other man enquired, speaking first. He was built sparely; his eyes were a faded blue. He wore northern-style chaps over black jeans and a lined black leather coat.

'No,' Casey replied very carefully.

'I didn't think so,' the stranger said, briefly removing his hat to wipe back his thinning blond hair. 'Trouble is, I never have seen him.'

'Neither have I,' Casey said honestly.

'You've heard the name before, though – Gervase McCoy?'

'I've heard it,' Casey admitted, still alert for any trouble that might be lurking.

The stranger nodded, lifted himself a little from the saddle and rubbed the insides of his legs. 'Do you mind if we step down for a minute? I feel like I've been aboard this nag for half my life.'

'All right,' Casey said carefully.

'I can boil up some coffee in a few minutes,' the stranger said, swinging from the saddle. 'If it suits you?'

'Suits me,' Casey said, still mistrustfully.

The man nodded, went to his pack animal and quickly found a coffee pot and a sack of ground beans. The men broke up a few pine twigs, piled them together, and with snowmelt for water, started the coffee boiling.

Crouching beside the fire, the stranger said, 'You seem a little uneasy, friend? Been Indian trouble up this way?'

'Not that I know of. They say the Nez Perce have mostly gone up to Canada and the Lakota have ridden south following the buffalo.'

'Well, that's what we were hoping. You never know out here, do you?' The stranger poured them each a cup of coffee and went on amiably enough, 'I'm Bill Hampton. Point man for Reese-Fargo Shipping. That name doesn't mean anything to you, I can see that.' The stranger smiled at Casey. 'Reese-Fargo has a contract with the army for bringing supplies upriver to the posts in the north country. Fort Union, Fort Peck, and our last stop, Fort Benton.'

'Upriver. . . ?' Casey inquired, not quite understanding.

'That's right. You can't haul army supplies overland. In this country! At this time of year! Reese-Fargo is a riverboat company, Mr . . didn't get your name.'

'Casey.'

'Casey,' the man nodded, finishing his coffee. 'The thing is, at this time of year we can't get our riverboats through either! The river ices up and there's no decent landing near Benton. Besides,' he added, 'the river's dangerously shallow at that point. The army's desperate to bring in supplies before the real Montana blizzards begin. Abandoning the fort is no option, since you never know when the Cheyenne or Sioux might decide to raid again and burn Fort Benton to the ground. They've done it once before. The army needs its supplies, and that's the business of Reese-Fargo.'

'You say your job is as "point man" for the riverboat company, and that you're looking for McCoy,' Casey said thoughtfully, adding the dregs of his coffee cup to the embers of the small smoky fire they had built. 'Do you mind if I ask what exactly it is that your position entails?'

Bill Hampton laughed pleasantly. 'No, not at all. It's no secret, Casey. I told you that our riverboats can't reach Fort Benton once true winter sets in. The river freezes and is far too shallow. There's no decent landing there. This man McCoy has contracted to construct a settlement at the last deep-water bend in the Little Missouri. From there, freight wagons can easily make the last leg of the trip to the fort. I just haven't been able to find McCoy!' Hampton laughed again. 'Of course I'm two or three days ahead of schedule – we didn't want to risk an early freeze, either. But I could find no sign of the building site, no trace of McCoy. I'm on my way to Fort Benton now to wait for him to arrive and explain matters.'

'I see,' Casey said slowly.

'Do you? It's fairly complicated; I hope I've explained it clearly,' Bill Hampton said; rising once again,.

'I believe you have,' Casey answered. 'I believe you have explained it all too well.'

Bill Hampton still wore a vaguely puzzled expression as he again mounted his sorrel and, leading his pack horse, resumed his ride to the north. Casey watched the riverboat agent for a minute before swinging into Checkers's saddle. He rode on with a greater sense of urgency, and stronger anger, but with more confidence. He need only to reach the river and guide Checkers southward and he would surely find Sundown – for Hampton had indicated that he had already visited the location, finding no one there, and it was in the direction opposite to the one the Reese-Fargo man was now riding.

But there was no one there!

What had happened to the wagon train? Had the snow bogged them down that much, or had the raiders come again?

Hampton had unknowingly substantiated some of Casey's conjectures and had provided some new, vital information, all of it more than a little disturbing.

Upon reaching the Little Missouri, Casey swung down and again let Checkers drink his fill. The banks of the river were fringed with icicles. The smaller branches of the dormant willow trees were sheathed in ice. The river flowed past sluggishly, deep gray and muddy even where the sunlight fully struck it. Tall virgin pines crowded the riverbank. Here and there leafless sycamore trees stood, prepared to wait out the long winter. A single crow perched near the tip of a dark pine complained raucously about something.

Casey crouched, watching the horse drink, watching the river flow. All right, he thought. What do I really know?' McCoy had learned something about the Reese-Fargo army contracts from some unknown source. He had sent Joe Duggan out to Sundown to find a suitable site for a river landing. Duggan convinced Jason Landis that this new section of land was the place for the harassed settlers to emigrate to.

Why involve the settlers? There were several answers. They had legal right to the land, for one thing. If they were allowed to reach Sundown on time, McCoy would play hell trying to claim the land for himself. Another reason could be found in the person of the ill-fated Virgil Troupe, the freighter. What did Troupe have that McCoy did not? Freight wagons and tons of sawn lumber which was as valuable as gold out here where no sawmill existed. The lumber Troupe and the other settlers meant to start their town with could be equally as well used by McCoy to build his riverboat landing. Letting Troupe and his crew transfer the lumber to Sundown for McCoy's people was much easier than trying to steal the lumber and transport it themselves. And Troupe could always be gotten rid of later.

As he had been.

McCoy was cunning enough to know that if the wagons did not reach Sundown in six days, the land-hold reverted to the Territory. Then what was Mrs Troupe, widowed and with an infant at her breast, to do with the lumber? McCoy could have obtained it at almost any price he cared to name.

'These are evil men,' Casey said, taking Checkers's reins once again, following the river southward toward where he hoped to find Sundown.

Mentally, Casey reined in sharply, although he let Checkers continue to pick his way through the pine forest. He knew why the wagon train had halted.

Bill Hampton was on his way to meet Joe Duggan at Fort Benton. Why did he expect to find him there? Because McCoy, who was a devious but careful planner, would have assured the Reese-Fargo Company that Duggan, his representative would be there to meet Hampton. What reason could Duggan have given the other settlers to wait for him while he rode for the army post? Why, that was simple – Casey had thought of it himself – Joe, fed up with the delays, angry at the Shadow Riders, would bravely set off to contact the army and plead for their assistance in reaching Sundown.

Except the army was never going to come.

Joe Duggan had entirely different business at the fort in mind, securing McCoy's claim to Sundown and negotiating the riverboat company contract.

Casey felt his weariness slip away, his numb confusion turn to fury. He was right; he had to be. What sort of man was Gervase McCoy, driving the settlers from their land and now involving them in a plot to further enlarge his empire, even if it meant killing some of them as examples, or for strictly mercenary reasons like the killing of Virgil Troupe seemed to have been?

Duggan had convinced the settlers that they needed to halt the wagon train while he raced to the fort, the safety of the women and children being paramount, even more important than a parcel of land – they could always find new land. The red-bearded Mike Barrow, his associate, would have been left in charge to counsel patience and caution until Duggan could return with army troops.

Colonel Landis would have seen through this charade. Perhaps he had had his suspicions much earlier. Casey believed more than ever that the first raid by the Shadow Riders had been a smokescreen to murder Jason Landis. Considering the number of men McCoy had, they hadn't put up much of a battle in the attack once Landis went down.

The colonel might already have been wondering about Duggan and Barrow. Perhaps that was why he had chosen Casey as his new commander, a complete outsider who could be trusted more than long-time neighbors.

That Casey might never know. He could not guess if the colonel was still alive, able to tell him what he might have seen or suspected. He could only now try to keep the settlers from losing what they had labored for and dreamed of – their own land. He had to find the wagons, somehow break whatever hold Duggan and Barrow might have on the people there and convince them that they had to spur on toward their new landholding with all haste, because already the sun was lowering its head again, the shadows lengthening, and when the land settled into darkness there would be only one day left.

One day to Sundown.

As he rode on grimly through the deepening shadows, the heavy murmur of the river accompanying him on his ride, Casey found himself wondering – not for the first time – about Gervase McCoy. Who was he; what did he want? It seemed strange that he was not personally leading his men as important as this plan seemed to him. Underlings like Joe Duggan had been delegated even the most sensitive tasks: completing the agreement with Reese-Fargo, for instance. Did McCoy trust Duggan so much?

Casey wondered if McCoy was perhaps too old and

feeble for this sort of ride; if he was a cripple. Perhaps he just enjoyed sitting in some great leather chair, drinking brandy like some lofty chess-master putting the world through its paces at his every whim.

Bill Hampton had never seen McCoy, which was odd considering how important the negotiations seemed to be to both parties. Thinking back, Casey could not think of a single person who had so much as described McCoy to him. He shook his head and continued on at a slightly faster pace. He had had more than enough of puzzles for a while.

It was time to get down to the business at hand.

The river flowed on freely, at times snaking away from the trail Casey was following southward through the pines, at times near enough to lap at the bank within yards of him. Daylight was fading in the river valley, although on the open prairie it should hold for another few hours. He had to find the wagon train. At nightfall, presumably, there would be cooking fires lighted unless fear or caution caused the settlers to make a cold camp.

It would not matter. They were still a day's travel or more from the river. Halted in their tracks, they would lose all by delaying too long.

Casey saw the monument from the corner of his eye and held Checkers up. Frowning, he swung down to examine what he had found: a cairn of river stones four-feet high standing at the very edge of the river.

Casey walked to it and crouched down.

The corner of a dark-yellow item, its color unnatural in nature, could be seen protruding from between a tier of stacked stones. Casey carefully removed several of the rocks and managed to tug the object free. It was an oilskin packet containing a single piece of folded paper which Casey smoothed out on his knee. The writing on it read:

North-west corner of Sundown homestead. Surveyed and placed by Colonel Jason Landis. No other subsequent claim will be valid after this date.

Dated, signed, witnessed by Joe Duggan, it seemed to legalize the homesteaders' claim. Except they had not fulfilled the requirement that they take possession of the land!

Casey replaced the heavy oilskin envelope and rose to his feet, feeling exhilarated and defeated at once. He had found Sundown, but there were no settlers occupying it, and the following day their claim would fall back into legal limbo, into the status of open range. And Gervase McCoy had already made his plans to immediately claim the land for himself.

Casey rode on. There was a palpable gloom settling across the land. Behind him the evening sky was streaked with deep violet and a few tendrils of scarlet. Ahead, the shadows of the pines lengthened, deepened and pooled together. He raised his collar and tugged his hat down tightly. It was going to be another long, cold night.

Hour after hour passed as Checkers trudged patiently eastward. The land spread out before him might have been green and golden when the colonel had come upon it, but now it was deep in snow, featureless. Casey had slowed the weary Appaloosa to a walk, but its fatigue continued to deepen. Casey halted the big horse, patted its neck and let it blow. A flickering, twinkling object appeared before his eyes and Casey frowned, It was no brighter than a firefly, but where would you find fireflies in winter? Peering more intently into the distance, squinting his eyes in concentration, he saw a twin to the first sparkling object.

They were not near at hand, but far distant. Camp-fires. Casey tensed, half-rose in the stirrups as if that could help him to see better, farther. Then he settled back into the saddle and with a silent apology to Checkers, started on again. It was all he could do to contain his urge to rush toward the camp-fires, but to rush madly on would kill the horse under him. He would have to be patient, to take his time. Time, however, was one commodity they were rapidly running short of.

In another hour – or was it two? Casey had no way of knowing – he topped out a low knoll and found himself near enough to the dully flickering lights to be sure they were camp-fires. And around them, in the darkness, he could make out the indistinct shapes of gathered wagons.

Making his way down the snowy flank of the hill, Casey approached the camp with caution. He could now see that the fires had burned nearly to embers; it was a wonder he had been able to make them out at all, even in the dead of night. What flames still flickered painted the canvas tops of the wagons with wavering, smoky images. Checkers's hoofs seemed to fall over-loudly even against the churned-up earth.

A man with a rifle in his hands stepped from behind one of the wagons and called out softly, 'Stay still, friend. Who are you?'

'Casey Storm.'

'Storm. . . ?' the voice was deeply puzzled, 'We thought you abandoned the train days ago.'

'I'm back,' Casey replied. Now he swung down heavily from the Appaloosa's back and stood waiting in the darkness for his interrogator. The man who emerged out of deep shadows so that Casey could recognize him by the feeble firelight, proved to be the stout, uncertain Art Bailey.

'Is the colonel all right?' Casey asked. 'I need to see him.'

'I couldn't say he's all right,' Bailey answered, 'but he's alive. You know his wagon.'

'Who is it, Art?' a voice Casey recognized as

belonging to Doc asked from out of the darkness.

'Casey Storm, Doc,' Art answered.

'Uh-oh,' Casey heard Doc mutter, and he frowned deeply as he walked on toward the Landis wagon. He slipped in over the tailgate to find Marly kneeling beside her father, cooling his face with a damp cloth. She heard him and turned her head, her eyes wide and startled. By the dim lanternlight Casey could see those dark eyes soften and she rose, still holding the rag, to stand staring at him.

'I thought you'd gone, Casey.'

'What did I tell you when I left?' he asked, approaching her.

'1 know – but all sorts of things can go wrong in this life, can't they?' She was standing stock still, her eyes searching his. A faint rasping sound from the bed caused Casey to break his attention away. Colonel Landis's eyes were barely visible behind the slits of his puffed, bruised-appearing eyelids.

'Casey. . . ?' Landis said, beckoning with one finger.

'Yes, sir.' Casey handed his rifle to Marly and kneeled down beside the colonel.

'What news?' Landis asked as weakly as before.

'Too much to fill you in on just now,' Casey said with a shake of his head, 'and not much of it good: I did find Sundown, Colonel,' he went on. 'You know that tomorrow is the last day.'

'I know it . . . they voted to stop. To wait for the

army to arrive to save more murders, the lives of women and children from the raiders.'

'Yes. But there won't be any soldiers coming, sir.'

'Neither did I believe there would be,' Landis said with extreme weariness, 'but that's what the people wanted. Casey . . . who's behind it? I know we have traitors among us.'

'Joe Duggan,' Casey told him, 'and I think Mike Barrow.'

'I guessed as much . . . it's all lost, then. All lost, Casey.'

'I don't think it has to come to that,' Casey said, with a determination he did nor entirely feel. 'Talk to them. You're still wagon-master, Colonel. Or rather *I* still am, I suppose. Summon Doc, Art Bailey, Barrow, anyone else who has a vote in the matter. I believe, sir, I can still get us through to Sundown.'

'How can we possibly do it?' Marly asked, poking fingers through her unruly hair. 'Time is up, Casey!'

'It is not,' Casey responded firmly. He rose to his feet and told them both, 'We have until dawn. If we can talk everyone into hitching their teams – now – and we travel throughout the night, I think we can make it. They have to be made to understand that Duggan is not bringing cavalry soldiers back. It was only a pretext. He went to Fort Benton only to delay the wagon train as he takes care of some business for Gervase McCoy. Don't ask me how I know that – it's a long story – but I do know it for a fact.'

'I suspected something like that. . .' Landis said weakly. 'But what could I have done?'

'Nothing. Don't blame yourself.'

'Marly!'

'Yes, Father,' she answered, She had already bundled up in order to slip out and summon the leaders of the wagon train.

'You'll stay with me, won't you, Casey?' the colonel asked.

'1 think it's probably better if you talk to them by yourself.' He added, 'I haven't really made a lot of friends among them. Just point out that I'm here and Joe Duggan is gone. That might give them enough to think about.'

With that, Casey himself clambered down from the wagon. He had it in mind to first try to do something for Checkers – at least unsaddle him and rub him down even if he could find no feed. Let the colonel have his talk with the leaders of the wagon train. It might be enough to let them see the mistake they had made in stopping here at Joe Duggan's urging.

Returning to where he had left Checkers, Casey began leading the roughly used Appaloosa across the camp. Here and there he saw lanterns flicker on behind the canvas walls of the wagons, heard men grumbling, an occasional curse as they were summoned from their beds for the meeting.

She came from out of nowhere.

Holly Bates had not been there one moment and the next she was, her blonde hair streaming down across her shoulders. She held a heavy robe of some sort clutched at her throat. Starlight caught her blue eyes and she smiled deeply.

'I didn't expect to see you again, Casey.'

'That's what everyone keeps saying.'

She turned and walked along beside him as Casey led the horse. 'Do you know Jeff Dannover?' Holly asked. 'No matter. He's got some hay bales in his freight wagon. He won't miss what it will take to feed your horse.

'Then,' Holly said, with a sigh, 'we have to have a talk, Casey.' She paused, stepped in front of him and took both of his arms in her small hands.

'Do we?' he asked, looking down into her eyes.

She nodded. 'Yes, there are still some things you don't understand, though I suppose you've guessed plenty by now.'

Jeff Dannover was apparently at the meeting at the colonel's wagon. Most of an already broken bale of hay rested against the plank bed of Dannover's wagon. Using only his hands, Casey scooped out a pile of feed for Checkers who started nibbling at it immediately. Casey tethered Checkers to the wagon and turned to face Holly who had been watching patiently, silently in the chill of the night.

Tilting back his hat. Casey asked, 'Now then – what was it that you had to tell me?'

'It's a little complicated,' the blonde answered hesitantly, her eyes turning down briefly. 'And it's not something I care to talk about where anyone might overhear me.' She turned her head and lifted her chin toward a nearby snow-patched stand of pines. 'Let's walk away from prying eyes and curious ears.'

'All right,' Casey agreed. With his rifle in hand, he escorted Holly into the darkness of the pine shadows: Overhead, stars winked through the upper reaches of the tall trees. Holly was frowning as if she were still undecided. Finally she nodded with decisiveness and shrugged and sighed at once. Casey had leaned his rifle up against a tree after assuring himself that no ambushers lurked in the shadows. He let the girl gather her thoughts as the cold, chilling wind worked its way through the pines.

'I've made up my mind now,' Holly said finally. 'At first I wasn't sure I really wanted to tell you this, but it makes no difference, does it? Since I'm going to kill you as soon as I've finished talking.'

EIGHT

Casey could only stare at the beautiful, blonde-haired woman. In Holly's hand was a small nickel-plated pistol she had been carrying concealed in the folds of her robe. Starlight glinted off the deadly little weapon which was clenched firmly in her right hand.

'I suppose I should have known,' Casey said. He inched forward, but Holly's foot swept out, knocking his propped rifle to the ground where Casey could not reach it without diving toward it. His own revolver was in its holster, hidden behind the skirt of his coat. The girl's teeth had begun to chatter; there was a strange excitement in her eyes.

'You're out here in wild country you don't belong in. I should have guessed that you were working with McCoy,' Casey said. Astonishingly Holly began to laugh. To laugh wildly until there were tears in her eyes. Puzzled, Casey could only stare al her.

'Fool!' she spat. 'Don't you understand? I *am*

McCoy! There's a reason I'm out here, all right. To keep an eye on the gang of incompetents I've surrounded myself with. Half of them can't wipe their noses without instructions.

'My real name is Genevieve McCoy. Once I got into the business world I started to use "Gervase". All important papers I simply sign with "G. McCoy" to avoid any legal sticking points that might arise.'

'I still don't understand why you're doing this,' Casey said. The pistol in the young woman's hand was unwavering. She smiled humorlessly, perhaps reflecting, and then her sharp tone of voice returned.

'Money! Can that be so hard to understand? Do you have any idea how hard it is for a woman to make her way out on the plains? That's why I always send someone like Duggan to take care of the tasks of commerce. No one takes a female cattle buyer, a land speculator seriously. And I mean to be taken very seriously, Casey, I mean to have their respect even if it is surrogate respect.

'When my parents brought me out on to the long plains, Dad built a soddy like the thousands of others you see scattered around and about. That was what we had: the soddy, a garden and two horses. The Indians had more than we did, by far. When the first winter set in, the roof of the soddy began to sag, the cold winds to blow drift-snow up against the northern wall so that we couldn't even see outside on a bright day. One of my jobs was scraping away snow from the ground to look for frozen buffalo chips which I'd carry back to the house in my apron to use for cooking fuel.

'Mother, I believe, started to go mad early on. The smoky close confines of the house, the snow piled six to ten feet high in the yard, nothing to eat but the rawest sort of meals made chiefly from roots. A year to the day after we had arrived in Montana, Mother died. Just lay down and never rose again. We had to wait for the spring thaw to bury her.' Holly – Genevieve – fell into a dark reverie again. Overhead the tips of the pines swayed in the light breeze. The stars still shone. The moon was low on the horizon, painting the snow fields with a soft yellow sheen.

'The month after Mother was buried, Dad finally got what he had been expecting all that time – a small inheritance from a distant uncle. He rode off toward town, waving his hat merrily. It seemed as if we were going to have some kind of luck after all.

'Of course, Dad never did have a stroke of luck, poor or otherwise. Well, you've seen him now.'

'*I* have seen your father?' Casey asked in bewilderment. Genevieve smiled thinly.

'Oh, I thought you knew everything by now, Casey,' she said with a hint of mockery. 'I brought Dad with me. He's driving my wagon.

'The mute! The thin, pale man?'

'Yes, that's my Dad. Lester McCoy, by name. You

see,' she said, tossing her head so that the fall of golden hair rearranged itself charmingly, 'He had gone to town to purchase a few supplies for us, but he was lured into a frontier saloon. The word must have gotten around that he had a little money. There are always people willing to take advantage.'

Casey nodded his understanding.

'They caught him in a back alley and beat him savagely. I watched him hover near death for weeks. Finally he recovered enough to dress himself and do simple chores – but he was never able to talk again. Those men had crushed a vital portion of his skull.'

Genevieve continued. Her story might have brought an upwelling of sympathy if Casey wasn't well aware of what the girl had become.

'Some of the inheritance money had been set aside at home for future use. I went to the little hoard. I rode to Bismarck by myself. When I got there, I found a hotel room and bought the local newspaper. . . .'

'And then?' Casey prompted.

'Then I started to buy land! Busted landholdings, slivers of land here and there. I swore I would *never* be poor again. You can lose almost anything – you can be robbed, a bank can go under – but you cannot lose your land. I thought of buying cattle, but that would have to wait until later. As long as I had land, I had leverage. I cheated men; I lied to them; I hired thugs for a quart of whiskey each to run farmers off their property. I purchased a set of lawbooks when I was living in that hotel room. I still have them in the library in my big house. I pored over those at night, looking for new ways to get what I wanted.'

'More land?'

'Yes, and the power that goes with it! I've never sold a single square foot of property and I never will.'

'What got you interested in Sundown?' Casey asked. He continued to try to edge closer to the woman, but she was having none of it. The muzzle of her pistol remained steadily trained on him.

'It's obvious, isn't it? I knew about the contract the army had with Reese-Fargo. It is a part of my business to know everything that is going on where development is concerned. Think of the opportunity this presented me – the riverboat company needs to have facilities built. The boatmen need to have sleeping accommodation and prepared food when they arrive upriver. Freighters and wagons will have to be provided to transport matériel overland to Fort Benton.'

She went on, 'When the good weather arrives, soldiers on leave from the post will flood the town eager to spend their back pay. What is there for them to buy at Fort Benton? Where else can they spend their money within two hundred miles? Those men, too, will be fully accommodated, in every way possible. *Sundown* – whatever I choose to finally name it – will be a fully functioning town . . . and I will own every inch of land it sits on, every stick of wood it's built from.'

Casey shook his head heavily. Quietly he told Genevieve, 'You are a sad and pathetic little woman.'

'Me!' Genevieve said in astonishment. 'What about you, Casey? Pathetic, am I? You don't even own a horse. And those *friends* of yours have not offered you so much as the tiniest, roughest parcel of land along the river. I never could understand why you chose to throw your lot in with them, to fight for that ungrateful crowd.'

'No,' Casey said after a moment's sorrowful reflection, 'I don't suppose you could understand it. Tell me, Genevieve, why is it that you want to kill me.'

'Why?' She tossed her golden curls again. 'At times I think you're a clever man, Casey, at others I think you're no smarter than the fools I have working for me – all of those rough-riding men without enough sense or gumption to shoot you down. You are in my way, Casey, that's all. Word fairly flies through this camp. I know you want to try to make a midnight drive toward Sundown.'

'I doubt they'll agree to it,' he said honestly. 'I also seriously doubt that it can even be done.'

'I can't take that chance, Casey. I tried to convince you back down the trail that you were making a mistake. Funny,' she said, with a shadow of wistfulness, 'men almost always do what I tell them to do.'

'They'll catch on to you, Genevieve. When they

find me out here, dead, you standing over me with a gun.'

'It won't be that way, Casey. I've thought about it. Nobody in this camp likes you; I'm everybody's darling. You lured me out here and then you got rough. I'll be in pitiful condition when the shots summon the camp. Weeping, trembling, my robe half-torn away from me. They'll say it wasn't my fault, that it was lucky I had my pistol with me.

'Don't you see, Casey? I knew you were trouble from the first time I saw you. When the colonel appointed you wagon master I nearly panicked. Now you've shown up again.' She shrugged her shoulders, 'There's nothing else to do. Sorry.' She aimed the nickel-plated pistol and two shots, one on the heels of the other, rang out in the forest copse.

Casey flinched reflexively; put his hand to his chest. But he had not been hit. How could she miss at that range?

Because Genevieve had never fired her gun. No smoke curled from its muzzle.

Marly stepped out of the shadows with her father's pistol held loosely at her side. 'I didn't want to do that, Casey. I thought that maybe after she had talked herself out . . . I did *not* want to do that!'

She stepped to Casey then and wrapped her slender arms around his waist. He stroked her abundant dark hair as shouts rose down in the camp and the sounds of excited men rushing in their direction came clearly through the cold night.

'How much did you hear?' Casey asked, tilting his head back to look down at Marly.

'Almost all of it.'

'Good. Then if we can get the others to listen to what we have to say, perhaps we can get this wagon train moving west by midnight.'

'They must listen!' Marly said emphatically. She was clinging to the lapels of his coat. The pistol had fallen to the snowy ground.

'We'll see.'

'What you said to Holly – Genevieve – whatever her name is, was it true? That we probably have no chance of reaching Sundown overnight no matter what we do?'

'We'll see,' Casey said again, more doubtfully. He put his arm around Marly and they started from the pines as a band of armed men, fearing that the Shadow Riders had attacked once more, rushed toward them.

They were confronted angrily by settlers with drawn guns before they could make it far. One man rushed past them, discovered Holly's body and called back, 'Storm has killed the Bates girl!'

The mob surged forward in a fury. At the forefront was the red-bearded Mike Barrow, a shotgun leveled at Casey Storm's mid-section. Casey could pick out Doc and Art Bailey among the crowd, the others were faceless in the shadows of the pines. They had one thing in common: they were in a murderous rage. All around Casey were the sounds of vengeful anger. Mike Barrow egged them on.

'Get a rope! A man who would shoot down a woman—'

'He didn't do it!' Marly said, her voice a near-shriek. She placed herself protectively in front of Casey. 'I did it! I did it because she was trying to kill Casey. If you'll took under her body, you'll find the pistol she intended to use.'

The stout, confused Art Bailey stuttered a question. 'You, Marly? Why would you kill her? Why would Holly want to kill Casey Storm?'

The man who had slipped past them called from beside Holly's body. 'There's a pistol here, all right. On full cock, too.'

'What's that prove?' Mike Barrow demanded. 'She was probably trying to defend herself.'

'She was trying to murder me,' Casey said in a calm voice. 'After she told me the truth of things.'

'What are you talking about!' Barrow shouted wildly.

'You already know, Barrow, You were working for her. You and Joe Duggan.'

'You're crazy as hell. I hardly knew the woman.'

'You knew her well enough to follow every instruction she gave you,' Casey said. 'Even to murder.'

'Holly Bates?' Doc said in disbelief, 'Why that little girl—'

'Her name wasn't Holly Bates,' Marly said, spreading her arms pleading 'I know it; Casey knows it; Joe Duggan knows it; Mike Barrow knows it.'

'You've got a lot of imagination, Marly,' Mike Barrow said with a crooked sneer, 'What was this all about up here? A lover's triangle—'

'There's one other person who knows that wasn't her name. She was his daughter.' Casey's eyes shifted toward the pale, gaunt man who stood helplessly on the fringe of the group, his bony fingers clenching and unclenching. 'Isn't that so, Mr McCoy?' Casey asked the mute.

Lester McCoy's dismal eyes met Casey's and as the others watched him, he slowly nodded, pushed his way through the mob and went to where the beautiful woman lay spread against the cold earth.

'You called him McCoy?' Art Bailey asked.

'That's right. That's his name. Her name was Genevieve McCoy – Gervase for business purposes. Isn't that so, Barrow?'

'I don't know what you're talking about,' Mike Barrow said unconvincingly. The astonishment on his face at being suddenly found out was deep. He was obviously shaken.

'I think we'd better talk about this,' Doc said quietly.

'I think we had,' Casey agreed. Staggering, stumbling, Lester McCoy passed through them again, carrying the limp body of his daughter. His haunted eyes were unfocused, his speechless mouth agape. Tears streaked down his ghastly cheeks.

Guns were holstered. Even Mike Barrow let the muzzle of his shotgun lower.

The men started back toward the camp, but Casey halted them with a commanding voice. 'One minute. You've already met with the colonel. He's told you why I mean to make a midnight run toward Sundown. You didn't all agree; I didn't think you would. Now I – and Marly – are going to relate the rest of what we know – what McCoy admitted to me. It won't take long, because I'll keep it as short as I can so that we don't waste time that could better he spent making preparations. But if any of you, after listening to what we have to say, still wants to wait here for an army patrol that is never coming . . . God have mercy on your stubborn souls.'

Marly had retrieved Casey's rifle for him; now he levered in a round and pointed the weapon at Mike Barrow.

'You, Barrow, I'll give you one chance. Ride out of the camp now, before these people know you for what you are. After they've heard us out, it will be *you* they want to string up!'

Barrow did not even pause to answer. Growling a single curse, he spun away and started marching back toward the camp where his tethered pony awaited. The men in the mob frowned or shrugged their shoulders. It was obvious that there had to be something to what Casey was saying. Otherwise, why would the always obstinate Mike Barrow be so quick to take to his heels, to simply ride out alone on the long Montana plains?

'Do you think that was a mistake?' Marly asked in near whisper.

'I don't know.'

'You know he'll ride directly to the Shadow Riders' camp and tell them that we're pulling out.'

'I know it. I have a feeling they were planning on raiding the camp again tonight anyway, Marly. Joe Duggan – and he was in a position to know – said a lot of them were army deserters. I wonder if many of them still have their old uniforms. To these tired folks already expecting an army patrol from Fort Benton . . . well, would there be a better way to approach the camp without stirring up alarm?'

'We'd better get going,' Marly said, as a sudden shiver not caused by the freezing cold of the night crept over her.

Casey Storm condensed what Genevieve had told him and Marly had overheard into a few short paragraphs. There was no time for a long-winded explanation, nor to answer the questions many of the settlers still had.

They were once again near the Landis wagon and when Casey had finished speaking, a voice, quite unlike the weak one Jason Landis had been reduced to through fever and pain, boomed out.

'Casey!' the colonel hollered from his bed. 'We're wasting time. You men get your teams harnessed and hitched, ride with your weapons at the ready. We're going to Sundown!'

For a moment Casey thought that the old soldier was going to add, 'and that's an order', and he smiled down at Marly. Looking around the circle of gathered men he told them, 'You heard the colonel. Let's get moving.'

It did not take as long as Casey had feared to get the wagons ready to roll. Experienced hands performed familiar work rapidly. Casey considered asking them to wrap their trace chains in cloth to prevent tell-tale jingling, but that would only waste more time. Besides, the rising half-moon would illuminate them harshly against the snowfield so that they would be seen much farther away than they could be heard.

Casey took his place on the wagon seat beside Marly. She lifted a gloved hand to pat her unruly hair and asked, 'Aren't you going to ride Checkers?'

'Not unless it becomes necessary. He's done more than his share already.'

'You two quit chatting and get cracking!' a roaring voice from within the wagon ordered, and Casey grinned.

'It seems your patient is getting better.'

Disdaining the whip, Marly snapped the reins across the flanks of the four-horse team, and without enthusiasm they pulled the wagon forward on to the snow-covered prairie. There were no shouts or catcalls from the other wagons as usually occurred during this stage of a drive. A brooding silence had settled over them one and all.

As they passed the silent man with his dead daughter still held in his frail arms, he watched them from the side of the trail. Briefly, Casey instructed Marly to rein in. 'Lester! Get in the wagon. You can do nothing for her now.'

Lester McCoy's stared at Casey without comprehension. There was no light in his eyes. They were those of a dead man. Finally, Lester shook his head and turned away in the snow; his only destination seeming to be a distant home he could share finally with his daughter.

The wagons rolled on. Their general direction could be taken from the stars, but Casey had a surer method for finding Sundown without creeping along through the darkness. It had not snowed again since he had ridden Checkers back to the wagon train. Following the tracks in deep snow was easier than following the stars. Of course he had ridden over knolls and through stands of pine where the wagons could not travel, but they would do to set their general course, and they could always cut tracks on the other side of these obstacles. Also, Casey had traveled this trail less than twelve hours earlier. His memory was not yet that faded.

They made good time across the open land. By the time the moon was overhead, Casey figured that they were more than half way to Sundown. There was time; there was just enough time to reach the site by dawn when their claim would expire.

If only the horses held up, if none of the wagons broke an axle on an unseen boulder. . . .

Then they came again, once more charging down at the wagon train from a piney knoll.

The Shadow Riders were not about to give up so easily.

NINE

'Rein up, Marly!' Casey shouted, as he dove from the bench seat into the interior of the wagon.

The colonel, propped up on one elbow demanded, 'Aren't you going to make a run for it, Casey?'

'No, sir. What kind of shooting can we do from jouncing wagons at a run?'

'Very well,' the colonel said, dragging himself half erect. 'Toss me my rifle, Casey. I can't ride, I can hardly walk, but, by God, I can still hold my sights steady!'

The first shots rang out creasing the silence of the night. The far clouds in the velvet sky drifted over peacefully, but now heavy gunsmoke rose to obscure the stars. Scattered answering shots from the wagons sounded near at hand.

'Marly,' the colonel shouted, 'Get inside this wagon. Now!'

'I've got to hold the team, Father.' She called back

across her shoulder.

'Set the brake and tie those leathers. If they run, they run. I won't have you sitting like a target up there.'

Marly quickly did as she had been ordered, slid back into the wagon and bellied back beside Casey to peer over the tailgate. Muzzle flashes stabbed at the darkness, but in the night the targets offered by the Shadow Riders were indistinct. Harnessed horses reared up and whickered in panic as the bullets continued to fly, one singing off the metalwork of the Landis wagon. Casey's mouth was tight. Abruptly he made a decision and began to rise.

'Where are you going?' Marly asked fearfully.

'Out to meet them,' Casey answered. He stretched out a hand toward the slipknot Checkers had been fastened to the wagon with, happy that he had resaddled the Appaloosa for just such an emergency.

'You said you wouldn't!' Marly reminded him, her wide eyes desperate.

'I changed my mind,' he answered coldly.

Slipping to the ground as the bullets continued to fly in all directions, he mounted Checkers. Bending low across the withers, he slipped the colonel's Sharps .50 from its sheath and handed it up to Marly.

'Your father asked for this.'

Marly was astonished to hear the slow, scrabbling sounds behind her, feel a hand brush her leg. The colonel, his face a mask of anguish, had clawed his way out of his bed and across the wagon to join her. He took the rifle from Casey's hand and checked the loads.

'Go get 'em, boy,' Landis said, as he settled into a prone firing position. Marly saw Casey, his Henry repeater in his hand, whirl Checkers and start him away from the halted wagon train, disappearing in moments into the night. She thought: *I am surrounded by crazy men.*

Then the colonel touched off his first shot, the unmistakable roar of the buffalo gun echoing across the camp. Marly could not be sure above the tumult, but she thought that she heard one of the raiders cry out in pain on the heels of the shot.

She scooted away and seated herself in the corner of the wagon, her knees drawn up, her arms around them, watching both of her men charge defiantly into battle.

In a brief lull in the shooting, Marly heard a woman's voice shrieking. It was Virgil Troupe's wife, Emma, who must have been hunkered down protectively in front of her nursing infant. Emma screamed madly, although not with pain. She shouted to the skies, to the gods of this forlorn country. 'I can't take any more of this!'

The gunbattle continued to rage. Marly saw the off-wheel horse of one of the freight wagons sag to its knees and thrash against the snowy ground, tugging its harness mates backward, heard her father's rifle roar again. Then Marly bowed her forehead to her knees and wondered how much more of this she herself could take.

Reaching the pines, Casey had slowed Checkers. The gunfire reached him only as muted popping, muffled by distance and by the forest. The pines were not dense enough to conceal the sky, and Casey glanced at the broken shafts of moonlight filtering through the sheer uncertain clouds above the tips of the dark trees.

Marly had been right.

It had been a mistake to let Mike Barrow ride away from the wagon train. It was certain that he had found the camp of the Shadow Riders and convinced them that there must be a new urgency in the pursuit of the settlers, since if Casey Storm had his way, the wagon train might still make it to Sundown in time to prove up their claim.

They would have listened to him. Would he even tell them that 'Gervase McCoy' was dead? Probably not. Let them continue to envision a big payday from the boss who had been so generous thus far. No doubt Barrow had been thinking since the boss was dead, the land and all it could promise with the construction of a riverboat port and the building of a new town, left the property in *his* hands, his and Joe Duggan's.

It might have struck Barrow that it was even more important to halt the settlers than it had been before. For now he would imagine himself not simply as a hired gun, but as a soon-to-be wealthy landowner.

Checkers, slightly rested and fed now, was still not in top shape. Casey could tell by the way the Appy moved. He rode him slowly through the pines, alert for any sign of the Shadow Riders' camp. He didn't expect to ride across it, but it was possible. When they did return from their raid, though, he would follow them and have an unpleasant surprise waiting for them. It was time to fight a little rear-guard action.

The raiders had had it all their own way, attacking when and where they pleased. They had no fear of a counter-attack. Why would they? The group of settlers was not going to pursue the raiders leaving all their goods, their wagons, their women and children behind unprotected.

Casey considered one other matter. Who was to say that this was the last attack the Shadow Riders would risk? If they could not stop the wagon train, was it not possible that their next inspiration would be to try to drive the settlers off their landholding by brute force: sniping at men in the fields; burning any new structure almost as soon as it had been completed; killing livestock? Why would they stop now? It seemed unlikely that Barrow and Joe

Duggan who had so much invested in the scheme would simply give it up and ride away. Burning their wagons had not stopped them; the death of McCoy had not.

All right! If they would not withdraw voluntarily, it was time to send them scattering with the only sort of encouragement they understood.

By the moonlight through the pines, Casey came upon the tracks of a horse in the snow and he frowned as he pulled up to examine them. Then, before he had swung down to have a look, he recognized them for his own tracks, those he had left on his way from Sundown back toward the wagon train.

All the better. After he had taken care of business, he could follow these back across the pine knoll and quickly catch up with the wagons. And they would be rolling again – of this he had no doubt. For now the colonel, if not fit, was back to being nearly himself; and he would keep them on the move, trying to outrace the dawn to claim their landhold.

Casey marked the trail mentally. There was a pile of weather-cracked granite boulders with a broken, dead pine tilting precariously from it. He would have no difficulty returning to this spot.

Assuming he was able to return at all.

He crouched waiting in the stillness of the cold night, knowing that the Shadow Riders would be coming. They would want to make their way back to their night camp after expending as much ammunition as the situation required. They wouldn't want to risk a stand-up fight with the settlers, nor hunker down for a night battle – these were not their tactics. They struck and retreated like any other guerrilla force, wishing to inflict as many casualties as possible without risking their own necks.

The rifle fire had long since died away. The night was dead calm; no breeze swayed the pines in passing. It was a chill and stealthy night where hunting creatures stalked each other.

It was Casey's turn to stalk. He had settled down against the base of a solitary old cedar, sitting on his bearskin robe, watching the night pass, the moon rise and pale, the constant stars twinkle, when he was aware of the sounds of movement beyond and below him. He rose stiffly. His wounds were still far from healed.

The sounds grew nearer and became recognizable. Horses moving over frozen snow, creaking saddle leather, the jingle of bridle chains and spurs. Casey stood near to Checkers, his hand on its muzzle, ready to silence the Appy should it decide to blow.

Now, a quarter of a mile off, he could make out the dark silhouettes of half-a-dozen men making their way upslope from the flats below. They rode as silently as possible, but the night was so still that any sound drifted clearly across the emptiness. Light from the moon and close stars glinted off silver trappings on some of the horses' saddles and bridles and was reflected off the steel of rifles carried unsheathed across their saddlebows.

Casey let them file past, Shadow Riders in the forest night. He was certain they had a rough camp somewhere nearby because after all these miles, after all they had been promised by Gervase McCoy, these gunmen were not about to give up now and simply drift away. When the last man in the line had passed, Casey swung carefully aboard Checkers and walked the Appaloosa along in their wake.

It was no problem to keep up with them. These men and their horses were weary, moving slowly. He kept fifty and at times a hundred yards distance between them as he paralleled their trail. Their camp would not be far away either. Why would they choose a site far distant from their quarry?

The night continued cold and still. In the dark picket line of the pines, Casey rode from moon shadow to moon shadow. He heard nothing, no one ahead of him now. The raiders had bedded down, or were preparing to, stripping their horses of leather, grabbing a few bites of whatever they had left to eat, rolling out their ground sheets and blankets, having completed another pleasant evening of terrorizing the innocent.

Casey slowed Checkers still more. A huge horned

owl swept low, startling him as it flew heavily past on broad wings. Nothing moved. He heard no one speaking in muted tones. He judged that it was time to get busy. Swinging down once again, he unbuckled a saddle-bag and removed an extra box of .44-.40 cartridges, stuffed them into the pocket of his coat and slipped into the shadows, leaving Checkers tethered to a low-growing pine bough.

He walked upslope, his boots slipping on the frozen snow underfoot. The moon beamed down like a mocking eye, watching. Perhaps, he thought as he walked on, he was half-mad to attempt this. It's really not a good idea to walk up to the gates of Hell and start pounding on the door to challenge the Devil. But it was time. It had to be done. Dogged in his determination, he continued through the dark pines.

Something clicked to his right, downslope from his position. It was impossible to tell what the sound was. It reminded him of a whiskey bottle meeting the rim of a tin cup. It might have been; perhaps not. It made no difference; he had found the camp of the Shadow Riders.

He was now at a point where the side of the knoll had sloughed off at some time past, leaving a rocky granite ridge to overhang the valley below. There were no trees, no stunted shrubs growing on the bare ridge that he might use for cover, and so Casey went to hands and knees to ease himself along it. Peering over the rim of the tongue-shaped ledge he saw dark figures below, and he went to his belly, easing his way to the very edge of the outcropping.

By the light of the pale half-moon he could make out a string of a dozen horses, tethered together on a rope stretched between two pines. He was near enough to see one of these toss its head and stamp an impatient foot. Fifty feet this side of the ponies a jumble of men lay rolled up in their blankets, shifting positions uncomfortably, trying to sleep in the cold of the night. He could hear occasional grumbling, once a weary curse.

Where was the guard? These were not careless men. They were experienced fighters, probably ex-military. There would be a guard, or several of them, watching for intruders. Casey smiled thinly. The guards could hardly expect an attack from a ledge a hundred feet above their camp. Still, he would like to discover where the guards – the men with the ready rifles – had their positions. A few more silent minutes passed before Casey noticed a moving shadow, saw a man with a rifle in his hand fidget with his trousers and lean one-handed against a broken cedar tree.

That was one guard, then. It could be that they felt secure enough in their strength to believe they needed no more. Silently Casey slightly shifted his position, removed the box of spare cartridges from his pocket, thumbed it open and placed it on the snow-streaked granite beside him.

The horses first.

The ponies, dozing themselves, would be only loosely tied to the tether line, and if he startled them awake and there was no man there to calm them, Casey had no doubt that they would scatter out of panic. Catching them again in the long forest, saddling them, would not be an easy task for the Shadow Riders. And Casey intended to keep the men pinned down long enough to give the horses time for a good long run across the woodland.

Casey found himself grinning without meaning to as he levered a round into the breech of his Henry repeater. This might be a deadly game he was playing, but it was going to be a hell of a lot of fun while it lasted.

From his prone position Casey took in a slow breath and triggered off his first round. The exploding shell was incredibly loud in tbe night, the muzzle flash flame-bright. He had aimed at the ground behind the hocks of the dozing ponies and one horse, perhaps stung on the leg by ice fragments kicked out in angry shock. A second and a third, a fourth shot twisted from the barrel of the Henry. These sang off one of the pines where the tether had been loosely tied, spraying bark. A big bay horse reared up, tossing its head wildly in surprise. It managed to tear free of the tether as another animal, a lanky roan with a blaze and one white stocking also panicked, backed away, and yanked its reins free of the line. That was all it took.

In true herd fashion, the panic spread down the line of horses and the terror spread as surely as if they had caught the scent of wolves among them. Now they reared, kicked, veered, twisted, tossed their heads, and almost as one broke free of the tethering rope to rush away from the unseen threat, weaving their panicked way through the deep, moonlit forest.

Casey shifted his sights.

As he had expected, the lone guard had located the source of the trouble, spotted Casey's muzzle blast on the ridge above the camp. He heard the man shout something, point a finger and go to one knee to better aim his rifle. He was still beside the cedar tree, and Casey, more ready for the exchange than the Shadow Rider, fired three rapid shots in and around the raider, one of these tearing a huge chunk of meat from the old tree. The rifleman changed his mind about fighting in the open, yipped, and dove for cover. The raider might have been tagged by one of the bullets though Casey had not tried to shoot him dead. It was hard to be sure, and it was of no consequence to him at that moment.

The other Shadow Riders tried to rise from the tangle of their beds, grab for their weapons and return fire, but they were half-asleep, had no idea where the shots were coming from, and half of them were still unarmed. Casey continued to pepper the camp with rifle fire until the barrel of his Henry was hot. Then he calmly reloaded while the Shadow Riders took to their heels, nearly trampling one another as they fought their way toward the cover of the woods in wild retreat.

Casey eased his way back from the edge of the outcropping. This was the second time he had warned them to keep away from the settlers. Maybe this time the message would stick.

Walking back to where he had left Checkers, Casey untied the Appy and turned its head southward. He rode slowly through the night, the moon descending now, showing its face prettily through the tips of the pine trees. He found the stack of weathered boulders where the leaning pine grew, found his own tracks, made only the night before, and guided Checkers up and over the knoll toward Sundown on this last night.

Perhaps it was now ended, perhaps the settlers could now have the homes they longed for, deserved. After all, 'Gervase McCoy' was no more, and that meant there would be no more wages to be had, and once the Shadow Riders realized it, understood that there could be a deadly price to pay if they continued, they might see the sense in dispersing, satisfied to take whatever they had already earned and proceed to their next job. Perhaps.

Joe Duggan, Casey felt sure, would not quit. But

what could Duggan do now? The bag of tricks seemed empty.

Unless Genevieve McCoy had somehow managed to leave a legacy of evil behind her.

TEN

They had made it through. Coming down from the snowy knolls in the dawn light, Casey Storm saw the horses, tended by kids, lined up along the river-bank to drink their fill from the sparkling, quietly flowing waters of the river. The morning sky was flushed orange and pale crimson, the new snow shimmering silver in the light of the coming sun. The wagons were haphazardly circled, and at least three campfires were burning brightly. The settlers were gathered around these talking, laughing with relief, discussing their recent past while planning for their future.

Casey trailed in on the weary Appaloosa. The eyes that met his now were no longer hostile, and here and there a man raised a hand in greeting. He found the Landis wagon near the river, in the cool shade of a trio of wide-spreading oak trees. Swinging down from Checkers's back, he simply dropped the reins and walked stiffly toward the rear of the wagon. He hesitated, wondering many things. Was he even welcome now that the job had been completed? Was the colonel even alive? Did Marly feel. . . ?

'Are you going to stand out there all day!' the colonel's voice boomed and, grinning, Casey levered his weary body up into the wagon where he found Landis in his bed, Marly crouched beside him with a cup of coffee. Her wide eyes met his with deep pleasure as she rose and, as she came to him and placed her slender arms around his waist, all of his previous fears seemed foolish.

'We'll need another cup of coffee,' the colonel said. He stretched his wounded leg uncomfortably beneath the blankets and told Casey, 'Sit down,' as Marly exited through the box to go to their small camp-fire for more coffee.

'Have any luck?' Landis asked.

'I had a conversation with the Shadow Riders. Whether it did any good or not, only time will tell, sir. You got the wagons through – I knew you would.'

'I wasn't so sure myself,' Landis said quietly, sipping at his coffe. 'You know, Casey, that bellowing I do is all just for show. Something I learned in command school. Around the dinner table, women and kids, I'm not that way. Not at all. It's just that most men, whether they admit it or not, need to have someone in charge to tell them what to do. And the loudest voice is the most effective when people are standing around indecisively.'

'How's your leg?' Casey asked, as Marly, having slipped quietly back into the wagon bed, handed him a steaming cup of strong coffee.

'I don't know. Hurts like hell still. Doc is of the opinion that I ought to try to make it to Fort Benton and see the army surgeon there.'

'Will they take it off?'

'I don't know,' the colonel said soberly. 'I do know I can't go on like this – confined to a bed. By the way, now that I think of it: I'll never ride again, this I am sure of. If you and Checkers get along . . . well, keep him for your own, Casey.' There was a soft sadness in the colonel's eyes. Who knew how many trails Landis and Checkers had ridden together.

'I'd be honored,' Casey said sincerely.

'For now, you'd better see if Marly is in the mood to rustle you up some breakfast. You must be hungry. You two probably have things to talk about anyway.' Did they? Casey didn't know. It seemed he knew so little about women sometimes. It was only now that he realized that Marly's hair, tangled and twisted on the plains, was brushed into a shimmering fall, highlighted by the low rays of the sun. She must have caught his eyes on her.

'I finally found the time to unpack my hairbrush,' she said, looking down and away. Casey suspected that Marly had done it just for him, but he said nothing.

'Go on, you two,' Landis said wearily. 'Leave me alone to get some rest.'

'Yes, sir,' Casey said, rising. He had only barely reached his feet when the cry came from the camp.

'Incoming riders!'

'Please,' Marly whispered, 'not again. Not now!'

Outside, Casey found Doc, Jeff Dannover, Art Bailey and half-a-dozen other men standing in a silent circle. Their eyes and the hunch of their shoulders were those of defeated men who could endure no more.

'Joe Duggan's back,' Doc told Casey as he arrived; and indeed, lifting his eyes, Casey could see the dark-eyed, handsome man walking his horse toward them, a thin smile on his lips. He was flanked by two rough-looking men they did not recognize and, in the shadows of the tall pines along the snowy knoll above them, Casey saw another ten men patiently sitting their horses, waiting to be called into action.

'You still here?' Duggan snarled at Casey without swinging down from his horse. His hands were crossed on his saddle pommel. The thick-legged roan he rode blew steam and shifted its feet. The two men flanking Duggan had their coats unbuttoned, the skirts flipped back for easy access to their sidearms.

'The question is – why are you here, Duggan?' Casey asked. He stood with his legs slightly spread, his Henry rifle loose in his hand.

'We just came by to request politely that these people keep moving. This is now our land,' Duggan announced. From an inside coat pocket he withdrew a long envelope. 'Gervase McCoy's claim. Would you like to examine it?'

'No need to,' Casey said. 'I can think of two reasons why that claim's invalid off the top of my head. One – you can't have failed to notice that these people have taken possession of the land, and by doing so, they've abided by the requirements of the Homestead Act. Much as you and your men tried to keep them from arriving, here they are.'

Duggan's voice became cunning. 'A day late, Strong. They didn't make it on time. McCoy's claim will stand up. I've a dozen men to swear that you never arrived at all.'

'You're a black-heated turncoat!' Art Bailey shouted. 'Here we are and here we'll stay.'

'Not above ground,' Duggan promised darkly. 'McCoy's claim will prove to be the only valid one, as soon as you people hitch your teams and move on. I suggest you start as soon as possible. Otherwise,' Duggan promised, glancing toward the knoll where the Shadow Riders waited, 'my witnesses might get a little aggravated, and who knows what they might do if they get aggravated.'

'I'm damned if I've come all this way to run again . . .' Jeff Dannover spluttered. Casey placed a restraining hand on the mustached freighter's arm.

'Easy, Jeff,' he said. Duggan was basking in his smug confidence. The cold-eyed riders flanking him seemed to be equally savoring the moment. Casey was far from finished. He took a step nearer to Joe Duggan. 'That claim's no good, Joe.'

'It will be – and soon!' Duggan promised.

'No, never,' Casey said frankly. 'Gervase McCoy is dead. She was killed back along the trail.'

Doubt flickered across Joe Duggan's eyes and then doubt deepened into something darker and more dangerous. He could have doubted Casey's words, but when he had added that *she* had been killed back along the trail, Duggan knew that what he had been playing as a pat hand was possibly a busted flush. He looked around warily.

'Where's Holly?' he asked.

'I just told you, Joe,' Casey replied, and Duggan could see where the last card had fallen. Without Gervase McCoy, the land claim he held in his hand was only a worthless piece of paper. The dead can't claim land in Montana or any other place Casey knew of. The two men riding with him exchanged uneasy glances.

'It can't be!' Duggan said defiantly.

'It is, Joe. Mike Barrow can tell you the truth of it.'

'Mike, they tell me, was killed in a raid last night.' Duggan rubbed his eyes with thumb and forefinger, trying to think of a way to turn the tables, but he was no Genevieve McCoy and that sort of manipulation was beyond him. When his hand fell away from his face, he looked more angry than defeated, however. There was dark fury in his eyes and it was directed at Casey Storm.

'You're behind this, Storm!' he said, as if he had been unfairly treated. For a moment, Casey thought the handsome, dark-eyed man was going to go for his gun, and he tensed. But, as the standoff threatened to become a gunbattle, a voice from the north of the camp called out again, 'Incoming riders!'

All eyes turned that way. Casey saw no one at first; he did see a flurry of activity on the knoll beyond Duggan. Men there had turned their horses and spurred them into motion. Now Casey saw the blue uniform of the approaching men. At the same time Duggan's companions recognized the cavalrymen for what they were, and they yanked their ponies' heads around, turning them on their heels. Whipping them with their reins, stinging their mounts with rowels, these two charged back up the knoll in the tracks of their companions.

Joe Duggan's hand fell away from his holster. He watched the approaching soldiers bleakly for a moment before he let the envelope containing McCoy's claim fall to the snowy earth. His sorrel trampled over the papers as Duggan rode off slowly, angling away from the Shadow Riders as if he did not wish to face their possible wrath. He had led them a long way, promised them much and delivered nothing but deprivation. No, they would not be pleased with Joe Duggan.

Casey turned to face the inriders. Marly had appeared to stand at his side, so near that her shoulder was pressed against his arm.

A man Casey recognized lifted his hat and waved it. 'Hello, Casey!' Bill Hampton called out, 'anything new?'

What the Shadow Riders had assumed to be a contingent of cavalry from Fort Benton proved, in fact, to be only three men, two officers and a sergeant, riding with the man from the Reese-Fargo company. Of course, the outlaws could not know that there was not a full company of men behind these three and they didn't stick around to find out. Even if the raiders were not shot down in battle, the army would not treat the deserters with kindness. If captured they could expect only the favor of a last meal before a date with the firing squad.

The morning was cool, but the sun shone brightly and the wind had been reduced to a rustling breeze shifting the high branches of the trees. The company had assembled near the oaks behind the Landis wagon and introductions had been made. The commander of Fort Benton, Captain Demarest, was there along with a handsome blond lieutenant named Shores who wore the insignia of the army corps of engineers. Presumably, he was there to evaluate the proposed landing site. With them was a three-stripe sergeant called Pierce who stood by at an uneasy parade rest the entire time, his experienced eyes lifting occasionally to the knoll beyond the camp. Captain Demarest was speaking, his words chiefly addressed to the colonel, who had been provided with a wicker chair from one of the wagons.

'I believe Storm here and you have given me a fair enough outline of what has happened. Lieutenant Shores and Sergeant Pierce here have discovered the other three claim monuments and retrieved the notices you placed there, and all seems in perfect order.' The long-jawed officer went on, 'And obviously you are present on the land,' he said, in what might have been an attempt at a joke. 'I will have an entry made in my log to that effect in case some question should arise at a later date. Pierce?'

'I'll see to it, sir,' the sergeant said.

'That being the case, let's proceed with the business at hand.' Demarest leaned forward on the oak log where he and Lieutenant Shores were seated side by side and said to the colonel, 'The construction of the riverboat landing is highly important to the army. You, sir, can understand the imperatives of winter provisioning better than most.

'Mr Hampton, here, is anxious to speak to you all on the desire of the Reese-Fargo to rent, buy or lease enough property to build the facility they require.

He assures me that the recompense will be more than moderate.'

The captain waved a hand toward Bill Hampton, and he spoke to the settlers, his words falling more easily on the gathered men's ears.

'Casey has filled most of you in on what the riverboat company requires. It isn't much, really. Just a place we can safely dock our boats and transfer the supplies to freight wagons to carry them the last few miles to Fort Benton. We will require stables, of course, and a bunkhouse arrangement of some sort where both freighters and riverboat crews can have a hot meal and a night's sleep when they need it.'

Sensing an objection, Bill said hastily, 'Of course, your own homes, businesses and farms once they are marked-out and built will be strictly off-limits.'

'That *was* one matter that was a concern,' Art Bailey said.

When he added no more, Casey told Hampton and the army officers, 'The McCoy organization, as you may or may not know, intended to eventually build an entire town on the river-front complete with restaurants, hotels, saloons, gambling houses and bordellos. They wanted to profit not only off the rivermen and the freighters, but had hopes that such a town would lure soldiers from the post.'

'We don't want none of that,' the taciturn Bailey said.

'Nor do we,' Bill Hampton said 'We want our

crews to be contented – but sober and contented, not drunk and angry at having their wallets lifted here.'

'I couldn't express my agreement more sincerely,' Captain Demarest said. 'We have beer on the post and card games which I turn a blind eye to. I know the troopers would like to have more in the way of entertainment, but I need my men ready to fight, not wandering dark alleys in some wide-open town looking for trouble.'

Bill Hampton took over the proceedings again. 'We're all agreed, then. From the essentials we have to descend to the basics:

'We need lumber to proceed with our construction. This you have.'

'That lumber is for our homes, our barns!' Jeff Dannover protested, rising to his feet from the stump where he had been seated, silently listening. Bill lifted an appeasing hand.

'Of course, but here is what Reese-Fargo hopes to do. If you will agree to sell us enough lumber to construct a landing, new lumber can be shipped by the first riverboat to replace what has been sold, along with as much more as might be required for you to construct your homes. What you have brought overland is quite a bit, but when it runs out, you will face a new dilemma – how to obtain more.'

Bill said encouragingly, 'Sell us what we need now, and after the landing is constructed the riverboats can supply you with all the lumber and other goods you need from here on. This can only be mutually beneficial in the long run.'

Casey had been silent for a long while. Seated on the ground beside Marly, occasionally patting her hand, he had let the others have their say. He, after all, was really not a party to any of this. Now he struggled to his feet.

'Bill, the lumber doesn't belong to the company in common.'

'Oh?' Bill's smile fell away. The point-man for the riverboat company had been certain that his logic was winning the settlers over.

'No. It is all owned by a woman named Emma Troupe. Her husband was murdered along the trail. She's got a suckling babe and has been terribly distraught. I'm sure if she were spoken to gently,' he said, glancing at Marly, 'she would agree to come to terms with you. But the fact is that those three wagonloads of lumber are all hers.'

'You say she's distraught?' Bill Hampton asked. Perhaps he had a vision of a madwoman he must deal with.

'Yes, anyone would be. My thinking is, that rather than you deal with her directly at this point, it might be better for her to have someone she trusts, like Doc here, and Marly – a woman should be present – talk to her in private, explain that the reason Virgil Troupe invested all he had in that lumber, brought it all this way, was for only one reason: to build this town.'

'Do you think she'll listen to reason, Storm?' Captain Demarest asked, lifting his eyes to Casey's.

'I don't know her well enough to predict that, sir,' Casey answered. 'I know she's sad, alone, baby at her breast and utterly without wherewithal if the timber *isn't* sold, but when people are distressed they don't always think clearly. I did have one idea, however, on how you might be able to sweeten she deal.'

'Me?' the captain asked in surprise.

'There are a few farms around Fort Benton, are there not?'

'Half a dozen, nothing large or imposing. Why?'

Casey told him, 'I was thinking that if along with the cash money a little bonus could be thrown in to clinch the deal. . . . Sir, do you know anyone around who might have a milk cow they'd be willing to sell?'

ELEVEN

The weather held clear for the next few weeks. Sundown was beginning to resemble a community. The settlers' homes, most of them only half-completed, were scattered at comfortable intervals across the broad landhold. Most were prepared to hold out over the rest of a harsh winter and begin their spring planting in a few months. The lumber that had been sold to the Reese-Fargo Company had been put to good use constructing a landing for the riverboats, and they had begun a barracks for weary upriver sailors.

True to Bill Hampton's promise, necessary goods were upriver in far less time than any freighter – were any willing to risk the winter snows – could possibly have brought them overland.

'Funny the way things work out,' the colonel said to Casey on one bright morning as he sat in the wicker chair on his partially completed front porch.

'Back on the old homestead, I'm not sure we could have lasted another winter. Now we don't have to worry about our stores getting low, needing timber or coal. The long trek was almost worth it.'

'If not for the blood that was spilled,' Casey commented.

'If not for that.'

The surgeon from Fort Renton had reset the colonel's leg, and though it was still immobilized, resting now on a wooden crate as he talked with Casey, the pain was much diminished and there was even some hope that Landis would be able to walk again when the bones had knit.

Marly emerged from the house bringing coffee and cookies to them. The sunlight highlighted her long dark hair. She wore a pale-blue dress with lace at the collar and cuffs. Peace seemed to have lent her a new, vivacious sort of beauty. Her wide eyes were no longer fearful, but content and confident. Casey accepted the coffee without speaking.

They had spoken at length over the previous weeks, but it seemed now that there was nothing left to be said. Casey sat on the porch of the new house, watching the glint of the wide river as it made its slow way past the willow-clad shores. The sun held bright. Only here and there did a patch of snow remain.

After only a few more minutes, Casey rose and stretched and reached for his hat. Without a word he placed his coffee cup aside and started walking slowly toward the river. He knew they were back there watching him go, Marly with her hand on her father's shoulder. He had said nothing more because there was nothing to say.

The simple truth was that he did not belong. He had not chosen a life among these people; only chance had thrown him here. He knew none of them, not really. He suspected that many of them would be happy to see him go. He was not a farmer, a town-builder, a carpenter, miller or storekeeper. Checkers was fit and ready to ride, to ride far away toward that nameless, featureless destination Casey could not define but which continued, nevertheless, to exist as a compelling goal in his mind.

Awayness.

That was what Casey Storm required. Already the daily routine of Sundown depressed him. People moved about energetically, antlike, laughing and shouting good-naturedly to their neighbors. Their high spirits were understandable. They had come far, fighting their way through much difficulty to find their goal: a place to settle, to plant their crops, to raise families.

The problem was that these had never been Casey's goals. He had fallen in with the settlers, helped them in some small way, but Sundown had always been their ambition and hope, not his. What he wanted was. . . .

It was hell when you tried to name it, pin it down.

It was such an elusive, restless need. Walking on, he began to feel guilty once again. Marly was taking every possible step to encourage him to stay. Not with spoken words, but with the way she kept herself, cared for him. There were times when he felt like a heel, seeing her eyes from across the room, wishing for him to give some small sign that he would at least consider staying with them. And then what? If he ever did cave in to her quiet pleading? He would only grow restless again. Months, years down the line he would slip out in the morning mist, saddle his pony and be gone before she had risen from her bed. And when she rose, her heart would be broken.

Casey walked on, deep in troubled thought. The oak grove where he found himself shut out the sun, leaving him in cool shadow. He could hear the murmur of the river, but could not see it beyond the thicket of willow brush.

The tall man stepped out of the shelter of the trees to block his way. Despite the chill of the day, he was not wearing a coat over his red shirt. What he was wearing was a walnut-gripped Colt .44 low on his hip.

'Hello, Deveraux,' Casey Storm said. The gunman grinned at him.

'So you figured that out, too, did you?' Tad Chaney asked. The Cheyenne gunman shifted his feet slightly, a preparation Casey did not care for. The breeze rustled through the trees overhead, and distantly a river-bird cried.

'What took you so long to show up, Tad?' Casey asked the man who had shot him down in the street not so long ago.

'Little things. It's always the little things, Storm. A man back in Cheyenne got me angry. I didn't kill him, didn't even try to, knowing I had this job to do. I shot him through both feet just to give him a message. Damned if they didn't throw me in jail for sixty days. Can you beat that!'

'Whatever job you were sent to do is meaningless now, Tad. McCoy's dead. Mike Barrow is dead. Joe Duggun has fled for parts unknown.'

'Oh, I know that, Storm.' The lean gunman continued to smile. 'But you understand my business, don't you? When a man is paid to do a job, he does it. Or he doesn't get hired again. I'm holding two hundred dollars of Duggan's money given to me to kill the man who was wagonmaster for these sodbusters.'

'That wasn't me,' Casey answered stiffly.

'That's not what they tell me,' Tad Chaney responded. 'Matter of fact while I was still in jail I got a note from Joe Duggan. You were the man he named.'

'Leave it be, Tad. They're all dead or gone. Pocket that two hundred and ride out. No one will ever know.

'*I'll* know,' Tad Chaney said, his voice gathering menace. 'And you would. Maybe some night you'll have a drink too many and start telling it around how you backed Tad Chaney down. Then I would have to come back for you. Don't you see how it is, Storm?'

'No,' Casey said honestly, 'I don't.'

The day held silent; they were as isolated as if they had been on the moon. The loon cried again from the river. Chaney shifted his feet again, only slightly, but he was ready now, that was clear.

'So long, Storm,' the gunman muttered, 'unless you've gotten a lot better since you left Cheyenne.'

Astonishing Casey, Tad drew first. His movement was fluid, rapid and Casey saw the muzzle of Tad's Colt issue red-gold flames as a .44 slug slammed into his body beneath the collarbone, spinning him half around. Perhaps the impact of that first bullet saved his life, because as Casey pawed for his own sidearm, Tad's second bullet, intended for Casey's heart, missed, ripping through the back of Casey's buffalo coat to groove a searing wound across his back.

Casey was already staggering, and now his knees folded up as he struggled to draw his own weapon, and his face slammed into the half-frozen earth beneath the trees. Bent in half, he brought his revolver up under his left arm and fired with desperate randomness. The bullet sang off into the trees, doing no damage.

Casey could hear Tad, still muttering something, approaching him where he lay. Casey flopped over on to his back and fired directly upward. His bullet caught the Cheyenne gunman beneath the chin as he stood over Casey with his pistol ready to finish the job. Tad Chaney flung out his arms and staggered back, his eyes puzzled, the lower half of his face nearly gone. Tad raised his revolver again, but he did not have the strength left to force muscle and sinews to obey his command to kill.

Tad simply folded up, going to his knees and then flopping on to his side to lie still against the ground, his gun inches away from his deadly fingers. Casey studied the man in awe. Tad Chaney could not be killed. He was too tough to die. Everyone said that. Casey felt like dragging himself to Tad's body and whispering into his ear – 'You see, no one's that tough,' but then the shock began to set in and he found that he could not rise. Nor could he crawl or call out for help. He had been right, he thought as he lay curled against the cold ground, blood leaking from his wounds, his own world spinning slowly away into darkness. *I was right, Tad.*

No one is that tough.

There was a bustle and a fuss and the hushed voices of people around him. Casey opened one eye, winced as sunlight struck it and closed it again. 'Draw the curtains,' someone said. After a few minutes Casey opened his eyes again to find Doc hovering over him, his mouth grim with determination.

Casey was lying on a bed; how he had gotten there

he did not know. Peering into the now-shadowed room he recognized it as the half-finished bedroom of the Landis house. In the doorway he saw the colonel, leaning on a crutch, his face creased with concern. And Marly!

Yes, Marly was there, doing something at a basin in the corner. She turned hopeful eyes toward him and resumed her work.

'Who was it, son?' the colonel asked, as Doc finished tying a knot in a bandage across Casey's chest and shoulder.

'Deveraux,' Casey managed to say through parched lips.

'I wondered what had happened to him.'

'Scat, Colonel,' Doc said sharply. 'You're not helping any.'

'You're right, Doc,' Landis agreed. 'And it looks to me as if you've done about all that you can do for now, too. Why don't you join me on the porch and let the healing begin?'

Doc nodded, rising from his task. The colonel hobbled from the room, Doc behind him. Marly remained behind. She smiled fleetingly, weakly, as she approached the bed and seated herself in the chair Doc had just vacated. She waved a hand around the room and said, speaking in a nervous, rushed voice, 'Once we get it painted it's going to be fine.' Looking at the curtains which fluttered in the cool breeze, she told him, 'Bill Hampton has promised to try to ship us some window glass on the next boat upriver. That will make a difference.' She sat with her head half-bowed, her fingers interlaced. Casey managed to mutter:

'Bill's a good man.'

'Yes he is, he really is. As a matter of fact, Casey,' Marly said hesitantly, her eyes still turned down. 'I spoke to him just this afternoon. He told me that when you're well . . . if you were interested . . . he could offer you a job as guide for the freight wagons through to Fort Benton. I mean if you would be interested!' she finished with a rush.

'I'd have to think about it,' Casey said, from behind closed eyelids. He was hurting, yet also drowsy. He wondered if Doc had administered morphine.

'Not only that,' Marly continued brightly. She was now on her knees beside his bed, holding his hand. Casey could see the dampness in those wide hopeful eyes of hers. 'I talked to Captain Demarest. There might even be an opening for you as an army scout . . . I mean, I know you have to keep moving, Casey, that you need to be out in the open, roaming free. I am trying. . . .' Her voice broke and now she began to sob softly, clinging to his hand with both of hers.

'I am trying to find some work that you would like to do, Casey! Some place to be that would make you happy.'

He tried to lift her hand to kiss it, but found he did

not have the strength to do even that just then. Instead he smiled and told her, 'I think I have already found that place, Marly. I suppose I was too blind to realize it, but I know now that I have finally found it.'

Marly bowed her head and continued to hold his hand as Casey closed his eyes again to sleep away the pain and his foolish doubts.